Aileen

Whispers of Destiny

Don D. Boucher

Editing & Interior Design by Silvestra Z. Griffin

Published by Parker Publishers

7345 W Sand Lake RD, STE 210 Office 3266 Orlando, FL 32819

Our books may be purchased in bulk for promotional, educational, or business use.

Please contact Parker Publishers at +1(689) 219-8883 or by email at contact@parkerpublishers.com

First Edition 2026

ISBN:

Dedicated to my late mom and dad, Alice, and Cecil Boucher.

They always believed in me. I know I was a handful.

Table of Contents

Aileen

Whispers of Destiny

Prologue

The story of Aileen Byrne begins in Applewood, Maine, a remote, fog-draped coastal village where the ways of life are directed by the tides and the cry of gulls. At the heart of this serene population is Aileen, a sharp, fiercely intelligent 13-year-old with a striking shock of vibrant, copper-red hair.

Her narrative revolves around a profound, almost mystical challenge: her deep-seated need to decipher a seemingly external influence, a soft, persistent voice, a powerful, protective feeling, or an uncanny intuition—that has subtly guided her through minor dangers and pivotal moments of her young life. She is driven by a quest for truth, believing that with sheer luck tempered by relentless perseverance, she will eventually uncover the source of this ethereal guidance, finally connecting with the mysterious entity that watches over her path.

Aileen's foundation is her family, starting with her father, Liam Byrne, a robust and dependable 35-year-old. Liam embodies the spirit of public service in Applewood as a devoted firefighter whose demanding career requires long, unpredictable shifts spent safeguarding the community at the local fire station. Of proud Irish descent, his ginger hair mirrors the same rich, fiery hue as Aileen's locks. Beyond the red curls, Aileen is very much his daughter, inheriting his bedrock traits: the perseverance that tackles any obstacle, the insatiable curiosity that drives learning, a contagious good humor, and a genuine, unwavering friendliness that makes him universally liked. Counterbalancing Liam's external duties is Aileen's 33-year-old mother, Faith. She is the essential operational nerve center of the household—a tireless stay-at-home mom who ensures the home runs with meticulous efficiency.

And then, there is eight-year-old Sean, Aileen's younger brother, a whirlwind of kinetic energy who is often described as a handful. Sean is perpetually on the hunt for mischief, plagued by a short attention span that causes his imaginative mind to wander rapidly from one fleeting thought or half-baked scheme to the next, guaranteeing a constant low-level chaos that keeps Faith firmly on her toes.

Finally, a long-lasting friend to Aileen, Maya Fielding stood as an unwavering constant in her life, their bond forged in the shared sandbox stories and whispered classroom secrets of early childhood. More than just a classmate through every grade, Maya had always been Aileen's trusted confidant, the one person privy to her deepest fears, wildest dreams, and unspoken thoughts. Through the tumultuous currents of adolescence and the shifting sands of young adulthood, Maya remained the steady anchor, an irreplaceable presence who understood Aileen without needing a single word.

1

Wake Up!

It's Wednesday, mid-spring in Maine, U.S.A., and the April school vacation will soon be coming to an end. At a modest Cape Cod-style home on Main Street, there's movement in one of the upstairs bedrooms.

Aileen Byrne, thirteen and still fiercely protective of her weekend sleep, lay sprawled across her small bed, half tangled in her duvet. Her face was buried in a pillow, dead to the world, when a sudden beam of harsh morning sunlight shot straight through a thin gap in the blackout blind of her east-facing window. It hit her face like a spotlight. She winced, eyes still shut, letting out a low, irritated groan as the light forced its way past her eyelids.

Through the bothering mental fog, she registered the almost horizontal angle of the sun's initial rays. This told her, unequivocally, that it was early, the kind of early where the world outside was just beginning to stir, a silence still presiding.

She didn't move at first, indulging in the sweet inertia of early-dawn slumber, trying to will the light away. But curiosity, or perhaps the complete disruption of her rest, eventually won.

Her green eyes, slowly clearing, began a lazy scan of the familiar bedroom, cataloging the reassuring presence of her dresser, her cluttered desk, and a stack of well-loved books, just to confirm she hadn't drifted back into a particularly vivid dream. Her gaze finally settled, softening, on a small, calico-patterned lump tucked into the shadowed corner by her closet door. It was Patch, the family's tortoiseshell cat, curled into an impossibly tight, perfectly comfortable ball of contented sleep. "Well, someone looks comfortable, Patch," Aileen murmured to herself, her voice thick with sleep and affection. "How long have you been there, hmm?"

The subtle shift from deep slumber to a hazy morning awareness began gently, rather than with the jarring clang of an alarm. Her eyes, still heavy-lidded and reluctant to fully cooperate, first registered the familiar silhouette across the room. Draped with elegant precision over the back of the antique vanity chair, the smooth, rich crepe of her black formal dress hung perfectly pristine, a silent testament to her careful preparation the night before. It was a classic sheath, cut to flatter, and its gentle flow hinted at the quality of the fabric, reflecting the faint, emerging light of morning.

A quick, sleepy scan of her immediate surroundings confirmed that everything else was largely in its rightful place – the neat stack of magazines on the bedside table, the carefully folded throw blanket at the foot of the bed. Everything, that is, except for the delicate, strapped black heels she remembered kicking off somewhere in the general vicinity of the closet after a long evening. Locating them had been a task she'd, quite deliberately, postponed until morning, a minor inconvenience for her future, more-awake self.

With a slow, deliberate movement that felt like pushing through thick water, she brought her hands up to her face. Her fingertips gently massaged her eyelids, rubbing away the last vestiges of sleep. A deep breath filled her lungs as the mental fog began its slow retreat, and clarity began to seep in. Yes, she was here. Fully, undeniably, consciously present in her own bed, in her own room.

A low, satisfying groan escaped her lips as she extended her arms high above her head, feeling the delicious pull along her spine and the satisfying crackle in her shoulders. "Ahhh!" she murmured, the sound a soft, private exhalation of contentment. Her mouth stretched wide in a jaw-popping yawn, eyes watering slightly, a final, full-body declaration of her transition from dreamland to wakefulness.

With renewed purpose, she turned her head to the left, looking straight toward the familiar arrangement of her nightstand. There, bathed in the faint, early morning light filtering through the curtains, sat her elegant reading lamp, a half-empty glass of water, and, most importantly, the glowing digital display of her alarm clock. The bright, red numerals stared back at her: 7:52 AM. Not too early, not too late. Just about right for a gentle start to this solemn day, a quiet moment before the world outside demanded her full attention.

Today was the day her family, dressed in black, would gather at St. Joseph's Church — the old brick building everyone in town knew — to do the one thing none of them wanted to do: say goodbye. It was for the funeral of her maternal grandmother, Nora Kelly, a woman who had graced the earth for a remarkable ninety-seven years before slipping away peace- fully just a few days prior. The news had been anticipated, yet it still delivered a heavy blow.

For the past few months, her parents had started slipping little warnings into their weekly updates after visiting. "Nana hasn't been doing too great at the nursing home, Aileen," her mother, Faith, would say quietly, her voice carrying a sadness she tried to hide. "She's really worn out. We just want you to be ready for what might happen." The words settled between them like a euphemism for the inevitable decline of a life lived long and fully. Aileen had nodded along, a knot forming in her stomach, acknowledging the grim reality that her beloved Nana's time was drawing to a close.

Aileen harbored a distinct aversion to churches and the solemn, often suffocating, rituals of funerals.

She felt pervasively uncomfortable whenever she stepped inside a church, a feeling that intensified to profound discomfort at funerals. The stillness of the place, the smell of old hymn books mixed with fading flowers, always made her feel light-headed, her skin damp with a cold sweat.

But beyond the physical sickness, it was the raw, unrestrained grief laid bare at memorial services that truly exposed her, leaving her feeling utterly vulnerable and overwhelmed, as if the fragile shield around her own emotions had been violently ripped away, forcing her to confront the stark finality of life and the terrifying fragility of existence.

The deep-seated yearning to say a final, heartfelt goodbye to her favorite grandmother, to the woman whose warmth had been a constant in her life, superseded any discomfort. Besides, she knew the weight of guilt would be unbearable if she failed to show up, a silent, disapproving shadow, especially when standing shoulder-to-shoulder with her grieving mother and the rest of her tight-knit family for this solemn occasion.

"Nana," as Aileen had affectionately called her since childhood, was more than just a grandmother; she was a great source of support and joy to her. A sweet old woman whose face crinkled with an easy smile that reached her bright, kind eyes, always seeming to radiate contentment. Her default setting was 'good mood,' a rare and precious quality that made her presence a comfort to everyone around her. It was no exaggeration to say that everyone loved her—from the nursing home staff who praised her gentle nature, to the neighborhood children who adored her stories, to her sprawling family who cherished her unconditional affection.

Aileen's mind went back a few years to one visit at the nursing home. The sharp smell of disinfectant and the low silence in the hallways felt completely wrong compared to Nana's lively nature. During that visit, while everyone was talking quietly, Nana had slipped her hand into the pocket of her cardigan and, with a playful glint in her eyes, pressed a small folded piece of paper into Aileen's palm as if it were a secret. "Read this when you get home, dear," she'd whispered, her voice surprisingly firm, "and in private... OK?"

Aileen's heart had given a small leap of excitement and anticipation. She'd nodded, a silent promise passing between them, and tucked the mysterious note into the pocket of her jeans, the crinkle of the paper a secret comfort against her thigh. Later that particular evening, back in the familiar refuge of her own bedroom, Aileen had retrieved the note. Her fingers trembled slightly with curiosity as she unfolded the small square of paper. Her brow furrowed for a moment, then softened into a wide, unbidden smile. It wasn't a profound message, no grand parting words, no hidden instructions or family secrets. Just a simple, perfectly rendered quirky little smiley face drawn with a sturdy black pen.

No words, no cryptic symbols, nothing else to decipher. The sheer, unexpected simplicity of it, so utterly Nana, brought a wave of warmth washing over Aileen. She didn't question it, didn't try to find a deeper meaning beyond the obvious message of pure, unadulterated joy. She just smiled, a genuine, heartfelt smile that reached her own eyes, and carefully placed that precious note into a small, cedar-wood box.

This particular box, burnished with age, resided in the top drawer of her dresser, a silent repository for items that held immense, almost sacred, meaning for her. She had curated a collection of small, tangible whispers from her past

- a smooth, sea-worn pebble, a faded photograph, a tiny, intricately carved bird.

She would open the box occasionally, especially when the weight of the world felt a little too heavy, and gaze at these small treasures. Each one, especially Nana's unexpectedly weirdly-drawn smiley face, served as a quiet, potent pick-me-up, a gentle reminder of love, simplicity, and the enduring good in the world. And today, as she prepared to say goodbye, that smiling face whispered its comfort once more.

Today, though, with a soft groan that was more a vibration than a sound, Aileen begrudgingly began the arduous process of leaving the snug cocoon of her bed. She rolled over with a sigh, her body protesting the shift from warmth, and with a decisive flick of her arm, flung the heavy duvet and tangled sheets off her form.

Slowly, as if each fiber of her being resisted the inevitable, she swung her legs from the reassuring warmth of the mattress, letting her bare feet tentatively touch down onto the shockingly cool kiss of the aged pine floorboards. A shiver traced its way up her spine.

Her pale blue cotton nightgown, once meant for comfort, was now creased and twisted around her waist and shoulders — clear proof of a night spent turning restlessly. She stretched out her stiff limbs, a little unsteady at first, then stood and paused for a moment, trying to steady herself in the stillness of the morning.

With a practiced gesture, she smoothed down the creases of her nightie, adjusted the twisted shoulder strap, and then, still half-sleepwalking, ambled towards the window. Her fingers found the pull cord of the roller shade, and with a soft snap and a whir, she sent it retracting upward.

As the shade zipped out of the way, the room was instantly flooded with a golden invitation of morning light. The sun, a brilliant orb in the eastern sky, lit up her face, banishing the last vestiges of sleep-fog, and its gentle caress felt immediately warm and awakening on her skin, chasing away the chill from the floorboards. She blinked, her eyes adjusting, and then took in the expansive vista outside.

The sky was an unbroken, vibrant blue, utterly devoid of even a whisper of a cloud. Below, a symphony of bird activity was already in full swing. Chickadees flitted through the evergreen boughs with frantic energy, robins hopped across dew-kissed grass in the distance, and the distinctive cries of seagulls echoed from the shoreline as they busily searched for their breakfast among the trees surrounding the sleepy coastal village.

Her modest home was at a relatively short distance from the charming little Applewood cove that cut into the rugged, rocky shoreline.

From her window, she could not only view the birds darting through the wind-swept pines and broad-leafed trees but also watch the bolder gulls and terns swooping with precision, diving down towards the sparkling water beyond her view.

Then, her gaze caught something unexpectedly majestic: a bald eagle, a regal silhouette against the brilliant blue, soaring high up in the sky, performing effortless circles as it patrolled the terrain below, the undisputed monarch of the morning.

With a slow, almost theatrical drag of her feet, Aileen finally ambled towards her dresser and its oval-shaped mirror. Her reflection greeted her with a wild disarray of her sleep-tousled red hair and green eyes still a little bit puffy.

A glimmer of mischief sparkled as she leaned closer, a familiar morning ritual taking hold. She made a comically exaggerated face at herself, a sort of whimsical challenge to the day. Tongue out. Eyes crossed. Head tilted. Ridiculous—but it worked, making her look like a character straight out of a silent film.

It was just Aileen being herself, the inimitable, and silly as usual, always injecting a touch of playful rebellion into the mundane. She'd then reach for the small comfort of her plush, fuzzy slippers, wiggling her toes into their warmth, and with a soft, padded rhythm, wandered out of her bedroom door, the promise of a nice breakfast and the day ahead beckoning.

Aileen's feet, still slightly heavy with the last vestiges of sleep, carried her efficiently into the cool, tiled sanctuary of the upstairs bathroom. It was a quick stop, a routine born of years and the unspoken urgency of a morning that, despite its solemn undertones, still demanded its usual rituals. She went through the motions she knew by heart, then reached for the brush on the counter. With a few decisive, sweeping strokes, she tamed the gentle disarray of her ginger hair, pulling it back from her face until it lay smooth and manageable.

Before leaving, a small, almost unconscious gesture, her palm cupped against her mouth, a quick exhalation, then a sniff – a silent, self-vetted approval that her breath wouldn't scare anyone off. Satisfied, she turned from the mirror, its surface reflecting a determined but still-soft gaze, and made her way through the hushed landing, down the familiar wooden steps, drawn by the distant murmur of voices and the faint, comforting aroma of coffee and toast.

The kitchen, already bathed in the pale, nascent light of a new day filtering through the large bay window, was a hive of activity. Her father, Liam, stood in the corner, a striking figure even in the relaxed attire of a charcoal t-shirt stretched comfortably across his broad chest and faded gray sweatpants. At thirty-five, Liam was the epitome of a local hero, his tall, muscular frame testified years spent battling blazes and rescuing lives as a firefighter. Today, on his day off, the usual intensity in his eyes was softened, replaced by a thoughtful watchfulness as he observed his family. A gentle smile played on his lips as he saw each person engaged in their own regular routine – pouring cereal, setting cups, or simply lost in thought.

This morning was different. A significant, somber punctuation mark in their lives: the funeral for her beloved grandmother, her mother's mother, was scheduled for later. The next few hours, therefore, were a precious buffer, a time for the family to gather not just for breakfast, but to gather their thoughts, to share unspoken comfort, and to brace themselves emotionally before the inevitable, final goodbyes.

From the first-floor bathroom and laundry room down the hall, Aileen could distinctly hear the gentle, off-key humming of her mother, Faith, a sound lost into the rhythmic swish of water and the thud of the washing machine. It was a sound Aileen knew intimately, a private soundtrack to their daily routines.

Aileen felt an especial, almost telepathic bond with Faith, and that familiar hum, usually an indicator of calm contentment, now resonated with a peculiar, soft lightness. Despite the profound gravity of the day, Aileen sensed a quiet, almost serene mood emanating from her mother. It wasn't happiness, not in the traditional sense, but something akin to peaceful acceptance.

Aileen knew, with a certainty that only a daughter could possess, that her mother had been bracing herself for this loss for a long, protracted while. The protracted, agonizing decline, the slow erosion of life, had been difficult for everyone, but most of all for Faith. Now, in the quiet hum, Aileen perceived a profound, if bittersweet, relief—the suffering was over, and her grandmother was, finally, at peace.

The morning light, still soft and tinged with the cool blue of dawn, filtered through the kitchen window, illuminating the breakfast table where Aileen's younger brother, Sean, already sat. Eight years old and a perpetual whirlwind of energy, Sean had a knack for finding, or more often creating, mischief, especially when the quiet of a new day threatened to leave him unoccupied. His unruly blonde hair, perpetually tousled, seemed to mirror the playful chaos he often brought.

Currently, his attention was singularly focused on a bowl of crispy O's floating in milk. He wasn't just eating them; he was engaged in an intricate engineering project. With the side of his spoon, he meticulously pushed individual pieces up the bowl's interior curve, his brow furrowed in concentration. The goal: to see precisely how far above the milk's surface he could coax them, balancing precariously on the rim without gravity claiming them, sending them tumbling back into the milky depths or, worse, scattering onto the clean tabletop.

Aileen, observing from the doorway, a wistful sigh escaping her lips, couldn't help but smile faintly. "Everything is a game to him," she thought, a familiar weariness mixing with a trace of fond exasperation as she slowly shook her head from side to side, a silent, habitual gesture born of years of sibling antics.

With a gentle scrape, Aileen pulled out her chair at her usual spot and settled down. Her dad, turned from the counter. "Morning, sweetie," he asked warmly, "Pancakes or eggs for breakfast this morning? I could whip something up." The tempting aroma of maple syrup and sizzling bacon seemed to hang in the air, a phantom conjured by his words, but Aileen felt little appetite. "Oh, Dad, thank you, but I'm not all that hungry," she replied, her voice a little softer than usual. "Just a little bit of cereal today, with a small glass of orange juice, please."

Her dad, a man polished with time and experiences, nodded without a word, sensing the underlying current beneath her polite refusal. He moved to the pine cupboard, the familiar click of its latch breaking the silence, and retrieved a ceramic bowl, a gleaming spoon, and a small, sturdy tumbler for her juice.

He then presented her with the family-sized box of frosted flakes, its colorful design not quite settling to the day's looming solemnity, allowing her to pour her own portion. She carefully measured out a modest amount, listening to the dry rattle of the flakes. Then, he took the tumbler, poured a steady stream of bright orange juice until it was half-full, the liquid sloshing cheerfully, and offered it to her with a gentle smile. "Good?" he asked, his eyes conveying more than the simple word. She met his gaze, offering a small, grateful nod.

As they ate in comparable quiet, her dad broke the silence again, his tone softening further. "How did you sleep last night, Aileen?" he inquired, his concern evident. She stirred her cereal idly. "Oh... okay, I guess," she admitted, a slight pause betraying her true feelings. "I tossed around some at first, my mind just wouldn't settle, but I finally managed to drift off and got a decent night's rest." A faint shadow crossed her features, quickly replaced by a wry smile. "The sun woke me this morning, though. Hit me right in my eyes, streaming through the window shade like a spotlight."

Her dad then cleared his throat, the lightheartedness of the conversation giving way to the day's somber reality. He looked around the table, addressing not just Aileen and Sean, but everyone around the house. "Just a reminder, everyone," he began, his voice firm but gentle, "Nana's funeral this morning is at 10 AM. We all need to be dressed and in the car, ready to go, by 9:30 AM sharp." He paused, letting the words sink in. "Since the church is just a short, five-minute ride from the house, we should arrive a bit early. That way, we'll have a chance to greet any other family or friends as they arrive, and spend a few moments before the service begins."

The playful clinking of Sean's spoon against his bowl instantly ceased as the weight of their dad's words settled over the breakfast table, a collective understanding of the day's seriousness replacing the morning's light hum.

Aileen pushed her almost-empty cereal bowl aside, a faint smile playing on her lips as her younger brother, Sean, continued to treat his breakfast more like a toy than a meal. Finished, she finally left the table, heading down the hallway where she paused to peek into the bathroom, offering a quick, warm smile to her mom who was busily folding clothes. Then Aileen climbed the stairs to her bedroom, where the day's preparations truly began. She made a brief detour to the upstairs bathroom to brush her teeth, before returning to her room at the end of the hall to find her favorite pair of shiny black, dressy shoes with the little bows.

These weren't everyday shoes; with their approximately 2-inch heels, they were reserved for special occasions like today, making her feel, and look, more grown-up and a little taller. As she slowly lowered herself to her knees to look more desperately into her closet, a fleeting thought crossed her mind, wondering why she hadn't had the foresight to retrieve them the night before when she'd laid out her dress.

Eventually, way out back, tucked in a corner under an old blouse that had slipped off its hanger, she located them. Grabbing one, then the other, she placed them on the floor beside her before standing up with her prized possessions.

Walking over to the window, she held them up to the sunlight, noticing they needed a good dusting. From her bottom dresser drawer, she pulled out an old, faded t-shirt, meticulously wiping every surface until the shoes gleamed almost new. "There, that's better!" she declared proudly, a satisfied smile spreading across her face, as she carefully set them down by the chair where her special dress awaited.

Glancing over at her nightstand, she peered at the alarm clock, and it read 8:45 AM, so that meant she had 3/4 hour to get ready.

Aileen shut her bedroom door, flipped the light switch that turns on the overhead light so she could see better, and proceeded to remove her nightgown. Then, grabbing the dress, she pulled it over her head, sliding her arms into the sleeves, and pulled the hem down to her knees. Walking over to the mirror in the corner where the cat was sleeping earlier, she examined herself and turned around to see all sides. She approved, nodded to herself, smiled, and said, "This will do nicely!"

Next, she stepped over to her dresser, glancing at the small, framed photo of her whole family, and then grabbed her hairbrush, along with two hairbands that she placed around her wrist. She managed to smooth out any lingering tangles and knots. Then, using a comb, created a center part and gathered her red hair into ponytails. The hairbands held her pigtails in place, and with a glance towards the mirror, she confirmed they were evenly spaced.

She then opened the top drawer of her dresser and located the small wooden box that held all of her jewelry, what there is of it, and picked out a set of gold hoop pierced earrings. She then went back to the mirror and stuck them in each earlobe. She had gotten her ears pierced way back when she was about five, so the earrings now went in without any trouble.

As she was getting ready, so was the rest of the family, in their way. Dad put on his nice shirt and tie, his sports jacket, and his freshly ironed pants, and dressy dark brown shoes. Mom wore her gray, frilly top and dark maroon slacks. Aileen's brother, on the other hand, was busy playing a video game on his tablet, disregarding the time altogether. He was winning, and it was hard to stop when you were winning, right?

Suddenly, Dad shouted, "Everyone almost ready? We're leaving in 10 minutes..."

Sean finally realized that he had been goofing off for too long, put down the tablet, and quickly threw on a blue and white striped collared shirt out of the closet, and dark blue jeans.

Five minutes later, Mom, now standing in the kitchen by the sink, yelled out, "Come on, guys, it's time!"

One after another, the rest of the family shuffled down into the kitchen as Mom inspected each one, making sure they were presentable for the solemn services. Once she gave the OK, they headed back down the hallway to the side exit by the driveway.

Each in turn filed out of the door, down a couple of steps, headed for the car that sat parked nearby in the driveway facing the street. Meanwhile, Dad, being the last one out, grabbed the car keys hanging on the hook and made doubly sure that the door was latched and locked. He proceeded out on the side porch, down the steps, and onto the driveway. Walking around the front of the car to the driver's side, he looked around, and, seeing that it was a partly cloudy day now, smiled, opened the car door wide, and seated himself behind the wheel and fastened his seat belt.

Confirming that everyone was in the vehicle, buckled up, and settled down, he put the key in the ignition and started up the car. He then placed the transmission lever into "Drive," pulled up the driveway to the street, looked left and right for oncoming traffic, and slowly maneuvered left out of the driveway. As they picked up speed, he said, "Here we go, guys."

2
The Funeral

The ride to the church began roughly parallel to the narrow ocean inlet, leading to the small cove where Applewood was established back in the early 1700s. Along this winding route, the road meandered past several small, weathered homes, sturdy lobster shacks, and a scattering of run-down buildings belonging to the local fishermen. These are the hardy folks who headed out before dawn each day to man their lobster traps and cast their fishing nets into the unpredictable depths. They are men and women forged by the sea, having weathered both the abundant hauls and the crushing storms, resilient in their spirit. God-fearing and grounded, they embodied a profound respect for the ocean, accepting what it yielded to sustain their families and their timeless way of life.

As the Byrne family proceeded east on Main Street, they caught brief glimpses of the cozy harbor, its blue waters shimmering between the scattered buildings that lined the southern side of the road. Their progression, however, was soon brought to a halt at the bustling intersection of Main Street and Ocean Avenue, a prominent corner in Applewood governed by a traffic signal. From this major crossroads, their route was clear: they would need to make a left turn onto Ocean Avenue, heading north out of town towards the church, which lay approximately a mile or so distant from this central junction.

From the busy downtown waterfront, where the docks had great activity, Ocean Avenue began its northward ascent, gracefully bisecting Main Street before cresting several low hills on its gradual journey out of Applewood. This scenic route ultimately pointed towards Garrison, the next town north, a tranquil rural community located approximately ten miles away. Slightly larger than Applewood, Garrison was known for its peaceful neighborhoods, offering a profound sense of quiet solitude for those seeking a serene escape. It also had the closest sporting arena and major medical facility.

At the heart of town lay a bustling intersection, distinct for hosting the area's only traffic signal — a small beacon of order amid the flow. From its northeast corner spread a charming, tree-lined community park, a green retreat complete with a quaint gazebo that often served as an impromptu stage for evening concerts or local plays. Scattered park benches invited weary passersby to rest and watch, while the air on warm summer weekends often carried the smell of freshly popped corn from a cheerful vendor. Young and old alike lined up for the buttery treat, sometimes sharing a few kernels with the pigeons and seagulls, adding to the gentle buzz of this beloved town center.

In the lively southwest corner of town stood the community drug and variety store, a welcoming sight beneath its bright red awning that stretched invitingly over the sidewalk. This well-loved spot doubled as a classic dairy fountain, where youngsters often gathered, their laughter echoing as they enjoyed an ice cream cone or sipped a thick, cold milkshake. Beyond the sweet treats, the store offered an assortment of goods — writing materials, postcards, calendars, games, hats, t-shirts, ice, and books. Both local kids hunting for the newest trinket and curious tourists looking for something unusual stepped inside, drawn by the hope of finding something that might catch their eye.

A short walk down Ocean Avenue from the drugstore led directly to the busy waterfront, a place full of movement and character. Here, visitors browsed for unique finds at the antique shop, treated themselves to sweets from the local confectionery, or simply watched fishermen load and unload their boats at the docks. The air rang with the sharp cries of seagulls darting over the water in search of a meal. Now and then, a kind crew member tossed a piece of fish or crab into the air, prompting the gulls to swoop down with quick precision and snatch their prize before it even touched the water.

From the cool depths, the sleek gray head of a harbor seal sometimes broke the surface. Its dark eyes held a quiet mystery — alert and intelligent — as it scanned the shoreline and the people watching. It was a familiar sight, as several of these creatures had made this stretch of coast their regular stop, their strong forms a reminder of the wild beauty of the sea.

With almost ritual patience, they patrolled the water's edge, their strong necks craning, always alert for any flash of silver from a passing fish or, more often, the chance of an easy meal from the shore.

It was a common and sometimes debated practice for visitors, captivated by the animals' charm and the thrill of seeing them up close, to toss bits of food into the water. Children and adults alike leaned over the railings or stood at the edge, cameras ready, watching in quiet anticipation.

The seals, with quick and fluid movements, then dived beneath the waves with a loud splash that never failed to draw gasps of delight and excited chatter from the crowd. After their brief displays and a well-earned meal, instinct eventually pulled them back.

With a final, steady look that seemed to hold a trace of the deep, they turned, their powerful bodies gliding through the water before they disappeared once more into the open sea, leaving only ripples and a few fading memories behind.

The other two corners at the traffic lights were mostly open grassy areas, perfect for schoolchildren to enjoy all kinds of activities. Here, kids might start a quick game of baseball or football, or simply find joy in flying a kite against the sky. The wide space also invited energetic games of tag, letting them burn off energy and stretch their legs. Adding to the area's charm and usefulness, several tall oak trees stood around the property, offering not only shade but also great hiding spots for a spirited game of hide-and-seek.

As the Byrne family neared the old brick-faced church, the calm Sunday morning was suddenly broken by the sharp wail of a siren that grew louder by the second. A bright red fire truck, shining even in the morning sun, raced toward them from the opposite direction, its lights flashing urgently. Liam, quick to react, pulled their car safely to the side of the road and called out with a grin, "Go get 'em, boys!" as the powerful vehicle roared past.

It was a familiar sight for Liam; the local fire station where he usually served stood just a couple of miles up Ocean Avenue. But that day he was off duty, having swapped shifts with a colleague. Later that afternoon, a phone call to the station confirmed what he had suspected — it had been another false alarm. "Kids, huh?" he said with a wry smile, shaking his head.

When they arrived at St. Joseph's, the old brick church that stood beside an open meadow, the Byrne family noticed a few vehicles already parked in the small lot. Sean pointed out a gray sedan in the corner, prompting his mom to exclaim, "Hey, there's Mr. Wilkins' car! Huh, I didn't expect to see him here. I'm glad he came, though." Mr. Wilkins, one of Sean's elementary school teachers, was known as the only one patient enough to put up with Sean's mischievous streak.

As they prepared to get out, Mom's eyes caught sight of a black hearse parked discreetly around the back of the church, as if it were trying to stay unseen before the service began.

When the car came to a stop in a parking spot by the front door of the modest, unassuming church, the family climbed out one by one and headed for the large, arched wooden doors. Stepping up onto the granite curb and down the gravel walkway, they paused for a moment to look across the open fields, where butterflies fluttered in the morning air.

The big arched doors, weathered and showing their age, still opened with a firm tug and a soft creak.

As the Byrne family stepped inside, the heavy wooden doors clicked shut behind them, shutting out the world outside. Aileen's gaze fell on the small table near the entrance, where several votive candles burned softly, their warm light a quiet contrast to the stillness of the church.

Farther into the nave, a few people sat toward the front, still and waiting. Mom walked slowly down the central aisle, her shoulders slightly hunched, a handkerchief pressed to her eyes. Sean's gaze moved over the pews until he spotted Mr. Wilkins sitting in a back corner, trying not to draw attention while still showing his respect. When their eyes met, Mr. Wilkins lifted a hand in a small wave. Sean returned the gesture with a faint smile and then followed his family quietly toward the front.

While her mom stopped to speak with a consoling friend seated near the front, Aileen continued alone and walked to the wooden coffin. She looked inside, her eyes falling on her Nana, whose gray, wavy hair had been brushed neatly, her arms folded across her chest, and her hands holding her rosary beads. Leaning over the edge, Aileen kissed her fingers, then touched her grandmother's cool forehead and whispered, "I love you, Nana, and I'll never forget you." A single tear slid down her cheek as she stepped back and turned to find a seat. A sudden chill passed through her, even though the mid-morning sun filled the room with warmth, but she told herself it was just the weight of the moment.

With tears gathering in her red eyes, her mom leaned over the casket and kissed her mother's forehead. "Bye, Mom. I love you and we'll all miss you," she whispered, her voice heavy with emotion, before turning away to join the rest of the family in the front pew. Aileen's dad followed, bowing his head in silent prayer before stepping back. True to form, Sean, always the procrastinator, wandered over last, looked down at his grandmother, and gave a quiet nod before returning to his seat. Settling beside Aileen, he asked softly, "She does look at peace, right?" Aileen nodded and gave him a small, reassuring smile.

A stillness settled over the room, broken only by the faint rustle of a turned Bible page or a muffled cough. Then, from the dim archway of the sacristy behind the altar, Father Paul appeared. His black cassock, freshly pressed, and his white Roman collar stood out sharply against the subdued tones of the mourners. He walked forward with steady, deliberate steps and took his place before the congregation.

His gaze moved slowly across the rows of bowed heads and tear-streaked faces. It wasn't just a glance; it was a quiet acknowledgment, a shared moment of grief. His eyes lingered for an extra second on the front pews where Nora Kelly's family sat, their sadness heavy in the air.

He drew a deep breath before he began, his voice calm and steady as he recited the opening prayers, each word clear and full of quiet strength that seemed to steady the room itself.

After the first prayer, his tone softened further—almost a whisper—yet it held the attention of everyone present. His voice carried both sorrow and warmth as he spoke about Nora Kelly's life. He mentioned her "rambunctious spirit," a phrase that brought faint smiles to some faces as they remembered her laughter and her boundless energy. He recalled her "big dreams," describing them as the stars she reached for, proof of her imagination and her steady belief in shaping her own future. He listed her many accomplishments not just as achievements, but as signs of her determination and kindness—shown both in her work and in the countless small ways she touched other people's lives.

He spoke of her "loving family," the foundation of her life — a circle of support and affection that shared her joys and now bore her loss. Finally, his voice fell to a near whisper, heavy with sadness, as he spoke the hard truth of her "untimely passing" — a life cut short, leaving behind a silence filled with questions and what might have been.

The last moments of the service came quietly. A few more prayers, spoken through unsteady voices, mingled with the sound of soft sniffles from the congregation. Brief, heartfelt words from family members followed, their memories and tributes blending sorrow with love — a final farewell spoken into the still air.

With steady, deliberate movements, the priest approached the open casket. He dipped a silver aspergillum into a small vessel of holy water and, with a gentle motion, sprinkled the polished surface — a simple blessing for the journey ahead. The droplets caught the light for a moment before disappearing, a quiet sign of farewell. Then, with a soft click, he closed the lid, the faint sound marking the end of a chapter. A quiet sigh passed through the mourners.

At a nod from the priest, everyone rose from their pews, the soft rustle of clothing filling the silence. Then, as if on cue, the great oak doors at the back of the church opened slowly. Six men, dressed in dark suits, entered with measured steps. They were the pallbearers — their faces solemn, their movements steady — a silent promise of respect and strength.

With practiced coordination, the pallbearers moved with quiet purpose, fanning out to encircle the polished dark oak casket where it rested on its low, velvet-covered stands. There was no need for words; a few exchanged glances and small nods were enough to show their shared understanding. One by one, they stepped into position, their movements steady and deliberate, hands reaching for the brass handles that lined the sides of the heavy casket. With a unified motion — strong yet careful — they lifted it together, the weight rising smoothly from its place until the dark wood hovered above the stands. For a moment, the room seemed to hold its breath, the empty velvet below marking the quiet transition from rest to farewell.

A deep silence fell over the congregation as the pallbearers, carrying their solemn burden, began their slow, measured walk down the central aisle. Each step was deliberate and respectful, echoing softly through the wide space of the church. Then, as if on cue, the low, steady tones of the organ rose to fill the air — a mournful melody that swelled and faded, its sound both sorrowful and strangely peaceful. The music carried through the arches and along the still pews, guiding the procession toward the bright light at the far doors.

In a quiet, steady line, the mourners followed. Close behind the casket walked the immediate family, their faces marked by grief, some leaning on one another for strength, their steps slow and heavy. Behind them came friends and others from the community — a gathering of shared lives and memories — forming a silent, moving stream that flowed toward the church's exit, accompanying their loved one on her final journey.

As the great wooden doors swung open, the pallbearers guided Aileen's grandmother's casket carefully down the front steps and out into the cold air, where a polished black hearse waited with its rear door open. With steady precision, they slid the casket into place before one of them closed the door and joined the others in the nearby black limousine, ready to lead the way to Lilac Valley Cemetery. Aileen and her family settled into their car, watching as the hearse and limo pulled away, then fell in behind, part of the quiet line of family and friends that followed in mourning.

As they drove through town, Aileen noticed how the sky had grown heavy with clouds, a gray expanse that seemed to reflect the weight in her heart. "Even the heavens are sad," she thought, the quiet words echoing the sorrow that filled the air. Ahead, the slow line of cars moved behind the hearse, their headlights glowing faintly through the dim light of the overcast day.

Almost at once, a hush of respect spread along the street. Other drivers, without needing direction, pulled over to the curb, their engines idling softly as they made way for the passing motorcade, giving space to the quiet dignity of its purpose.

When they arrived at Lilac Valley Cemetery, the procession of vehicles wound its way to a calm, tree-lined section set aside for Nora Kelly's burial. With practiced care, the pallbearers opened the hearse's rear door, lifted the wooden casket, and set it gently on the waiting mortuary lift positioned above the open grave. They then stepped back, standing still as the family and other mourners gathered beside it.

The priest's voice, low and steady, rose once more in prayer. He asked God to bless Nora, to forgive her faults, and to grant her peace. When the final words were spoken, the casket was lowered slowly into the vault, its descent marking the last farewell. As it came to rest, the lift straps were drawn back, and the cemetery workers, who had waited quietly nearby, removed the equipment and stepped aside, leaving Nora in her final place of rest.

One by one, they stepped forward to the mound of fresh earth beside the open grave, each family member taking a moment to speak their final words to the departed. A handful of soil, held tightly, was tossed onto the casket below, the soft thud marking the weight of farewell. When the last gestures of respect were made, they moved back from the graveside and slowly gathered into a quiet circle near their waiting cars.

There, beneath the whispering leaves and the faint sounds of the world beyond the cemetery, they shared stories of Nora Kelly — small memories, moments of laughter, and words of comfort that brought a fragile peace.

One by one, they embraced, their goodbyes filled with both sorrow and love.

At last, with everything that needed to be said spoken, they parted, climbing into their cars and trucks. With a few gentle waves from the windows, they drove away in different directions, leaving the stillness of Lilac Valley Cemetery behind them.

3

The Heads Up

The Byrne family's departure from Lilac Valley Cemetery was less an exit and more a solemn, hushed procession, the low hum of their dark sedan a faint counterpoint to the silence surrounding them. Inside the car, the air carried a shared, steady melancholy—a blend of recent sorrow and the acceptance that follows a final goodbye. Each face, marked by the day's weight, held a reflective sadness, eyes distant yet connected by an unspoken grief.

They understood, without a single word exchanged, the burden they carried—the legacy of loss, the widening void—and the simple comfort they now sought, hoping to piece themselves back together bit by bit.

The car, a quiet vessel, followed the narrow, winding road that curved past ancient headstones and drooping willows, each turn a slow departure from the sacred ground. Sunlight filtered through the thick canopy of oak and pine, casting brief patterns across the seats, mirroring the shifting emotions within.

The only sounds were the soft crunch of tires on gravel and the steady breath of the air conditioning in a space otherwise free of any expression of grief.

It wasn't until the sedan passed through the iron gates and turned onto the broader, more familiar stretch of Ocean Avenue that the spell began to lift. The transition was immediate—the distant rush of traffic, the sharper light of late morning, the sight of daily life unfolding beyond the cemetery walls.

In that moment, as the world shifted from muted reflection to ordinary motion, Aileen, seated in the back, leaned forward, her elbows resting on the console between the front seats.

Her voice, gentle with concern, broke the long silence as she reached toward her mother in the passenger seat. "Are you okay, Mom? I'm sure that must have been very traumatic for you." The words lingered, a quiet invitation to acknowledge the emotion beneath the surface.

Faith, startled slightly by the sound, turned her head, her movements slow and deliberate. Her eyes, still holding traces of the day's ordeal, met Aileen's, a silent exchange passing between them. With a steadying breath, Faith answered, her resolve clear despite the faint tremor in her hands. "Yes, it was. But now that it's over, I'll be okay in time." It was a promise to Aileen and to herself—a small declaration of strength in a world that had shifted.

The late-morning spring sun stretched long amber shadows across the familiar streets as their car—reliable but showing its years—moved down Ocean Avenue. This intersection, where the busy road met the quieter stretch of Main Street, was a fixture in Aileen's mental map of home, usually marked by its predictable rhythm of traffic and pedestrians.

But as they drew closer, something shifted. It wasn't a sound she heard with her ears, but an internal resonance, a presence brushing past her awareness like the flick of a moth's wings. Aileen felt a faint, almost imperceptible whisper at her ear—not a voice, exactly, but a pressure, a thought pressed straight into her mind.

Then the formless presence tightened into an urgent command: *You need to stop, now.* It was no louder than the rustle of leaves, yet it carried a sharp clarity, an instruction that bypassed logic entirely. The words—or whatever they were—landed in her consciousness with an icy certainty. A sudden chill swept along her arms, lifting the fine hairs on her skin, her body reacting before her mind could.

She nearly dismissed it as wind from the open window or a stray misfire in her nerves. Yet the insistence of the voice—its firm, quiet authority—held her attention. It came again: *Stop the car.* Not a suggestion, but an order, steady and unyielding, settling deep into her instincts.

A frantic, almost desperate plea tore from her throat before she could form a coherent thought. "Please, I need you to stop for a minute, Dad!" she blurted, the words rushing out, her voice higher and more strained than she expected. The sharpness of her own outburst startled her, sounding foreign in the still cabin, her urgency surprising even herself. Her breath hitched; a tremor ran through her.

Liam, her father—a man whose easy-going nature was often tested by Aileen's more eccentric quirks—reacted with characteristic calm. His silvering brows pulled together, a silent question in his steady blue eyes, but he didn't hesitate. Used to his daughter's sudden impulses—from abrupt detours to unexpected declarations—and wearing a look that blended confusion with affection, he guided the car toward the curb. The tires crunched on the gravel shoulder, bringing them to a halt several hundred feet before the busy intersection, as if something unseen had stopped them just in time.

A collective gasp filled the car as their attention snapped to the road ahead.

A sleek silver sedan, its driver likely pleased with shaving off a few seconds, sped past them. With the green light in his favor, he continued confidently down Ocean Avenue toward the harbor.

Then the world seemed to tilt.

From their right, racing east along Main Street, a massive black pickup—old, rust-eaten, and moving far too fast—appeared out of nowhere. It barreled through the intersection, ignoring the red light entirely, its engine roaring in open defiance.

There was no warning. No screech of brakes. No horn.

Only a brutal, sickening CRUNCH—so violent it felt like a punch to the chest. The truck plowed into the sedan's passenger side with devastating force. Metal twisted and shrieked, glass burst into a spray of glittering shards, and pieces of steel and plastic flew outward like shrapnel.

The smaller car, completely outmatched, was T-boned and spun across the asphalt like a crushed toy before collapsing in the middle of the intersection, steam and acrid smoke curling from its mangled frame.

Liam moved on instinct—the instinct drilled into him from years as a firefighter. His hand, trembling uncontrollably, closed around his cell phone. His voice, surprisingly steady despite the surge of adrenaline, spoke the familiar digits: "911." He reported the accident succinctly, giving their exact location, the types of vehicles involved, the visible damage, and the high likelihood of severe injuries.

His eyes flicked to Faith and Aileen, both frozen in shock, their faces drained of color. "Stay here," he said firmly, leaving no room for argument. "Don't move." Without waiting for a reply, he threw open his door. The quiet inside the car was instantly replaced by the harsh sounds outside—groaning metal, distant shouts, and the low hiss of leaking fluids.

He moved quickly toward the wreck, his mind running through first-aid protocols, every bit of training rising to the surface.

The smell hit him first: gasoline, burning oil, and something sharp in the cold air. Reaching the crushed silver sedan, Liam grimaced at the sight. The driver, a man in his late fifties, slumped against the shattered remains of his door, his face slick with blood. A deep wound along his forearm poured bright red across the twisted dashboard.

Liam pulled a clean folded handkerchief from his pocket and pressed it firmly over the wound, applying direct pressure. His heartbeat hammered against his ribs, but his hands remained steady, muscle memory taking over.

Then a new sound cut through the chaos—the rising wail of sirens. Police, fire, and ambulance units were racing toward them, the cries growing louder as they sped south down Ocean Avenue, a grim assurance that help was finally on its way.

Moments later, a fire truck—its red paint stark against the wreckage—came to a heavy stop, followed closely by a compact ambulance. Their flashing blue, red, and white lights washed over the scene, turning the street into a dizzying blur of motion and color.

As if rehearsed, the rear doors of the ambulance swung open with a sharp hiss. Two paramedics, identifiable by their dark uniforms and purposeful stride, stepped out. Their movements were fluid and precise. One, a man with a calm, focused expression, grabbed a large trauma bag, while his partner retrieved a rigid neck brace and a blood pressure cuff from another compartment. Without speaking, both assessed the scene in an instant and moved toward the mangled silver sedan where Liam knelt, still pressing firmly against the victim's bleeding arm.

Liam, his pulse still pounding hard from the adrenaline, quickly relayed what had happened. He described the sudden speed of the oncoming truck, the violent impact, and the moments that followed. Then, steadying his voice, he explained how he had found the driver and used his handkerchief as a makeshift compress to slow the bleeding.

The male medic met his eyes and gave a brief nod. "Alright, sir, we've got it from here," he said, calm and assured amid the flurry of movement. "You did an excellent job. Please step back and give us room." The message was clear: the situation was now in trained hands.

A deep, almost dizzying relief washed over Liam as the weight of responsibility began to ease. He pushed himself upright, his legs protesting after the long crouch, and moved back a few steps, watching the paramedics take over without hesitation.

As they began their rapid trauma assessment, a new set of flashing blue lights cut across the morning. A state trooper's dark blue cruiser rolled to a stop nearby, its siren now lowered to a soft pulse. A tall trooper stepped out, hat set perfectly straight, his eyes immediately scanning the scene. With practiced, deliberate movements, he started directing the growing line of cars and potential hazards around the accident perimeter. His presence brought an added layer of order to the unfolding chaos.

Liam, feeling a renewed sense of civic duty, approached the trooper, who acknowledged him with a brief nod. Once again, Liam recounted what he had witnessed, this time with less emotion, sticking to the facts of the collision and his immediate response. The trooper listened closely, jotting notes onto a small pad. "Thanks. You did good, sir," he said, his voice deep and gravelly. "Wreckers are on the way. They'll clear these vehicles soon, and we can get the road fully open again." His efficient, almost detached tone reinforced Liam's sense that the scene was now firmly in expert hands.

With emergency crews now coordinating everything, Liam allowed himself a moment to gather his scattered thoughts and slow his racing pulse. He took a deep, unsteady breath, the sharp smell of burnt rubber and spilled coolant still heavy in the cool morning air—a stark reminder of how close they had come to disaster.

Turning back toward their car, he saw it sitting a short distance away, a silent witness to the chaos. His family, though physically unharmed, was visibly shaken. Any earlier composure had evaporated the moment the sirens arrived. Faith had stayed near the car, her hands clasped tightly, her face marked by fear and overwhelming relief.

The moment their eyes met, something in her broke open. She rushed toward him, pulling him into a fierce, desperate embrace, burying her face in his shoulder. He held her just as tightly, feeling the tremors running through her—a shared reaction to what they had just survived. Over her shoulder, he caught sight of their children in the back seat, pale and wide-eyed, their hands pressed to the windows as they watched the surreal scene unfold—a jarring lesson in how quickly life can turn.

Aileen had never seen her father like this. The man who usually handled kitchen duties and weekend errands had shifted into something else entirely—a calm, decisive force, an anchor in the chaos of twisted metal and shattered glass.

His long years in the department had clearly given him an instinctive grasp of how to take command—to assess, anticipate, and act with a quick clarity that was astonishing to watch.

As the dust settled, both literally and figuratively, a strong wave of admiration washed over Aileen. It wasn't just pride in her dad; it was the sudden recognition of a side of him she'd never seen before. A wide, proud smile spread across her face, matching the warmth rising in her chest. Her thoughts, usually a jumble of teenage worries, narrowed into one stunned, heartfelt reaction: *"Wow, Dad. That was seriously cool."*

Liam, now regaining his composure, walked over to the children. His voice—low and steady—soothed the frayed nerves around him. He reassured them, explaining that everyone involved in the crash was being helped by the emergency crews and that the danger and chaos of the impact had passed. As he spoke, Aileen noticed the adrenaline that had fueled him slowly draining away, leaving behind a deep, unmistakable exhaustion.

His shoulders slumped slightly, and when he rubbed his hands together, she caught the faint tremor in them—a small but telling sign of the strain he had just endured. When he finally turned to her, his eyes still sharp with lingering intensity, and asked softly, "Are you alright, Aileen?" She managed a shaky, "Yeah. I just... I just want to go home now." The simple words carried all the shock, relief, and longing for normalcy that had settled over her.

Just as the trooper had predicted, the relative quiet of the scene was soon broken by the heavy rumble of two tow trucks arriving. Their massive engines idled as they pulled up, their hulking frames towering over the crushed vehicles.

Hydraulic flatbeds gleamed under the late-day light, ready to haul away the wreckage that had only moments earlier been functioning cars.

The injured driver—once the paramedics had stabilized him—was the first to be carefully extricated from what remained of his sedan. The rescue crew worked with slow, deliberate precision., their movements a practiced choreography of care and efficiency.

Then, he was gently lifted onto a waiting stretcher, his face pale against the white sheet, before being loaded into the back of the first ambulance.

Just as its doors closed, a second medical unit—lights already flashing—pulled up beside the pickup truck, its siren now silenced but its purpose unmistakable.

With swift, practiced movements, the crew surrounded the pickup truck, their actions coordinated and urgent. They assessed the driver, whose dazed state and visible injuries— including a rapidly swelling forehead and an arm bent at an unnatural angle—made the seriousness of the situation clear. Time was critical.

Working as a team, they secured his neck and spine, fitting him with a cervical collar and fastening him to a rigid backboard. The process was carried out with precision, every movement deliberate to avoid worsening any internal injuries that might not yet be visible.

Once immobilized, they lifted him onto a stretcher, several pairs of steady hands guiding the transfer. He was loaded into the back of the ambulance, the stretcher locking into place with a firm metallic click.

Moments later, the siren started up again, its piercing wail cutting through the midday noise. The ambulance accelerated quickly, red and blue lights flashing as it sped toward the nearest hospital in Garrison. Every second of the journey mattered.

Eventually, after the two wrecked vehicles were removed and the immediate chaos faded, the scene was left in stark relief. Shattered glass glittered across the asphalt, mingled with twisted metal and dark stains from leaking fluids marking the points of impact.

Distinct skid marks stretched across the pavement, stark evidence of sudden braking and violent impact. The sirens faded, replaced by an uneasy stillness interrupted only by the low murmur of police radios and the methodical movements of officers documenting the remaining evidence, their eyes sweeping over every detail. What lingered wasn't just the debris, but the lingering imprint of the collision—a grim reminder etched onto the road until the last shard was cleared by the town road crew and traffic slowly resumed.

Once everyone settled back into their seats, the click of seat belts sounded unnaturally loud in the hush. Liam gripped the steering wheel a little too tightly, his knuckles pale against the dark leather.

With a cautious glance around, he made the right turn onto the wider stretch of Main Street, the hum of the engine a steady counterpoint to the silence inside the car. Every instinct urged him to get them home—to the familiar safety of their own walls.

Back at the house, the moment the front door clicked shut behind them, a heavy quiet settled over the space. It wasn't just the lack of noise but a stillness that seemed to press in, dampening even their thoughts.

Each family member moved with a slow, almost detached heaviness, shrugging off coats and setting down bags as if burdened by something unseen. They didn't speak or look directly at one another, each caught in their own replay of what they had narrowly escaped—the screech of tires, the blare of horns, the crunch of metal, and the acrid trace of burnt rubber and fear.

Without a word, they drifted toward the living room and sank onto the sofa and armchairs, the familiar furniture offering little comfort against the turmoil still churning inside.

As she sat there, Aileen's mind refused to quiet. Flashes of the accident—twisting metal, shards of glass, the sheer ferocity of the pickup's impact—replayed behind her closed eyes, looping and jerking in impossible angles. Her thoughts spiraled not only around the tangible horror but the invisible force that had steered them away, that urgent whisper pressing her to act. It felt less like memory and more like proof of something beyond comprehension, an unseen hand threading itself through the morning, guiding them toward survival. Her chest tightened, pulse still too fast, and a chill lingered in her arms despite the safety of home. She wanted to analyze, to rationalize, to tell herself it was coincidence—but the certainty of that moment, the physical weight of instinct obeyed, refused dismissal.

She pictured her father, calm and commanding, stepping into the chaos with the practiced precision that had always been his hallmark. She saw Sean's shock and the way he had processed near-miss and mortality in staggered, trembling breaths. And she remembered the faint, ineffable whisper—so gentle, yet sharper than any scream—and the rush of relief that followed when instinct overrode fear. That memory pressed against her consciousness, intertwining with the terror and awe she felt for her family.

It was Sean who eventually shattered the fragile peace with his thin, almost reedy, voice that seemed to strain against the quiet. He had been staring blankly at the far wall, but a jolt, an almost physical tremor, passed through him.

He turned slowly, eyes wide and still unfocused from shock, and fixed on Aileen. A dawning, horrifying realization cut through the fog. "You know," he began, his words catching, throat suddenly dry, "it just hit me. If you hadn't felt the need to stop right then—if we hadn't pulled over at that exact, impossible moment..." He paused, swallowing hard, the image seared into his mind. "We would have been right in the middle of that intersection. That pickup truck," he whispered, voice trembling, "it ran the red light. Right where we could have been. Right where we would have been, Aileen. It could have been us."

Aileen, still piecing together her own fragmented memories, went pale. The blood seemed to drain from her face as the full weight of his words struck her. The inexplicable impulse that had made them pull over—the fleeting thought that saved them—felt like a small, miraculous intervention. Her breath caught, a cold shock radiating through her limbs.

Without thinking, she reached across the space between them, her hand finding Sean's and clutching it tightly, almost painfully. The unspoken *what if*—an entire world of loss and unimaginable tragedy—hung heavy in the air between them, a shared, silent anchor in the face of what might have been.

The air was thick with unspoken anxiety, making sleep a frustratingly elusive goal for everyone under the Byrne roof. The house became an uneasy symphony of restless family members: Sean kicked his covers off for the tenth time, Faith paced quietly in the hallway, and Liam's heavy sighs punctuated the silence from the master bedroom, the mattress springs groaning with each shift. As the hours dragged past 3 a.m., the individual struggles gradually subsided; the fretful whimpers softened into steady breaths, the pacing stopped, and the tension slowly eased.

Aileen tossed and turned, sleep a distant, mocking promise, constantly stolen by memories of that morning's bizarre experience. It wasn't just the accident itself, but the lingering premonition: that faint whisper she had almost dismissed, followed by the icy grip of an unexplainable feeling demanding they stop the car. Even hours later, the sensation clung to her like a phantom hand on her shoulder, leaving her wide awake and chilled to the bone.

Eventually, separately but almost simultaneously, the Byrne family surrendered to the quiet assurance of a long, much-needed rest, the stillness settling over the house like a heavy, calming blanket.

4

Close Call

Monday morning arrived soon enough with its familiar, insistent beat, pulling countless students from the lingering warmth of their Spring break and back into the structured world of academia. Alarms, once easily snoozed for the past week, now chimed with an undeniable authority, signaling the start of another school week. Backpacks, previously discarded in a corner, were now laden with textbooks and notebooks, ready for the day's lessons.

From quiet homes, a stream of students emerged, some grumbling softly about the early hour, others animatedly catching up with friends on the walk or bus ride, collectively starting on the journey back to classrooms and corridors, ready or not, for the challenges and discoveries that awaited them.

Trying to forget the tragic and weird events of last week, Aileen's footsteps echoed softly on the familiar linoleum floors as she finally returned to the bustling corridors of her junior high school. Though it's been only a short pause, it felt like an eternity since Spring break had started, and the scent of old books, fresh pencil shavings, and floor polish was a reassuring welcome.

Now, a proud eighth-grader, Aileen felt a fresh sense of purpose and excitement for the next couple of months. She genuinely liked school – the enjoyable challenge of picking up new lessons, the easy connection with friends laughing in the hallways, even the comforting routine of the day's familiar pace. This year, it wasn't just about getting through it; it was about savoring every moment, every discussion, every shared glance with a friend, as she stepped confidently into her final year before high school.

Classes began as usual, a routine buzz of learning filling the air. A dropped pencil here, a giggle there, everything seemed perfectly normal.

Ms. Davidson's voice, clear and engaging, guided them through the details of fractions, and Aileen diligently took notes, feeling a quiet satisfaction in understanding the complex concepts. The prior classes drifted by in a predictable pattern of reading, writing, and arithmetic. But then, an overlooked moment arrived.

The shrill, insistent ring of the morning recess bell pierced the calm, signaling freedom and recreation. Just as Aileen gathered her books, preparing to join the eager rush for the door, she heard it again – a faint, almost ethereal whisper, delicate as a breath, right beside her ear. It wasn't loud enough for anyone else to hear, nor did it sound like any voice she recognized. '*You must stay inside and help the teacher today,*' it seemed to murmur, a gentle yet firm suggestion that felt strangely compelling.

Aileen paused, a flicker of confusion crossing her face. Stay inside? When the swings beckoned? But before she could dismiss the odd sensation, Ms. Davidson, as if on cue, cleared her throat. "Aileen," she began, a kind smile on her face, "I wonder if you'd be a dear and help me with something. The whiteboard, I'm afraid, could use a thorough cleaning, please."

Aileen, still processing the strange whisper, felt a curious sense of affirmation. The request aligned perfectly with the mysterious prompt. A quiet determination settled over her, overriding her initial desire for recess. "Of course, Ms. Davidson," she replied in her steady voice. "I'd be happy to."

With a small, slightly wobbly step stool retrieved from the back of the classroom, Aileen began her task. The whiteboard, a vast expanse of dusty white, stretched from waist-high to almost to the ceiling. Using a felt eraser sprayed with a whiteboard cleaner, she started at the top, working her way down. The soft swish-swish of the dry eraser, accompanied by the fine film of dust settling on her clothing, was surprisingly meditative. Reaching the upper corners of the board required her to stand on the very top step of the stool, stretching her arm high above her head. It was right then, as she leaned slightly to wipe the top corner, that her gaze drifted towards the large window overlooking the venerable school playground area.

Framed like a vibrant painting, she saw her best friend, Maya Fielding, a whirl of bright yellow and laughter, soaring high on the swings. Her heart gave a little wistful tug in her chest. Aileen loved the swings, particularly the one Maya was enjoying, on the far right, the one nearest the red brick wall of the school building.

It was her deep personal belief, a secret theory she held close, but had never been proven, that this particular swing had chains just a little bit longer than the others. And because of that, she was convinced, it allowed her to pump her legs higher, to arc further into the sky, feeling a thrilling, momentary weightlessness that none of the other swings could quite replicate.

With a deep, steadying breath, Aileen resolutely pulled her eyes away from the vibrant scene outside. Her hand tightened on the eraser, the cool, slightly abrasive texture grounding her. The whiteboard, still streaked with the ghostly remnants of equations and forgotten diagrams, grabbed her attention again. It, after all, wouldn't clean itself, and this particular cleaning was more than just a chore; it was part of the preparation, a necessary ritual in a world suddenly teetering on an unseen precipice.

As Aileen carefully wiped away the last flaky remnants of dried marker, the faint chemical tang of the cleaner filling the suddenly still air, a familiar, if fleeting, sense of accomplishment settled over her. The once grimy surface now gleamed, a pristine white canvas. There was a rare solace in the tangible, in the simple satisfaction of a task completed, especially when the greater, unspoken task was so terrifyingly abstract.

Then, the classroom, previously bright with the morning sun, seemed to subtly dim, and she paused; a strange chill crept up her arms.

At first, a distant growl, like a slumbering beast, rumbled through the quiet morning air, eventually growing steadily louder and closer. She turned towards the window once more to check the sky outside just as a blinding, electric blue flash illuminated every corner of the room, followed milliseconds later by an earth-shattering BOOM that reverberated deep in her chest. The entire building seemed to shudder violently, windows rattling in their frames, and Aileen instinctively dropped the eraser, her heart leaping into her throat as the classroom lights flickered and died, plunging the room into an eerie twilight.

Aileen stepped down from the stool and onto the floor to regain her balance from that terrible jolt. She glanced over to the teacher, standing with her hands on her desk, and asked, "Are you okay, Ms. Davidson?" Ms. Davidson calmly replied with a nod of her head and said, "I am, thanks for asking!" Aileen gave her usual friendly smile, nodded and said, "Whoa, that was close!"

A collective sigh of relief rippled through the classroom as the old school generator finally kicked on, banishing the sudden dimness and coaxing the fluorescent lights back to their steady, familiar hum. But soon, the fragile calm was quickly shattered by a new sound – the distant, mournful wail of sirens.

They grew louder with alarming speed, their urgent cry unmistakably approaching the very grounds of the school. Her attention immediately drawn to the unsettling noise,

Aileen instinctively turned from the chalkboard and gazed out the filmy window. Her eyes widened slightly as she saw them: a huddled mass of figures, a crowd already gathered not by the main entrance, but over by the familiar, creaky swing set, watching attentively.

A sickening memory surfaced: her friend, Maya, laughing just moments before, on the swing set directly beneath the now-ominous sky. Without a second thought, Aileen launched herself away from the window, announced to Ms. Davidson, "I have to go!" as she burst out of the classroom, her desperate footsteps thudding down the hall and out the side door toward the playground.

Walking closer, her gaze swept wildly across the gathered crowd, searching, praying, until her eyes snagged on a splash of vivid color at the base of the swings. There, on the ground within a quiet, horrified cluster of bystanders, lay Maya in her crumpled, bright yellow dress she had worn to school that morning, a proof of the unthinkable. She had been struck!

Just as despair threatened to settle over the schoolyard, the wail of sirens signaled relief, and the ambulance, accompanied by a big red fire truck, rapidly pulled into the concrete expanse, coming to a halt near the swing set. A collective sigh swept through the anxious crowd, who instinctively recoiled to create space for the paramedics to reach Maya, still lying on the ground, her body trembling uncontrollably.

Swiftly assessing the situation, the medical team confirmed she was, thankfully, alive and breathing, though distinct burn marks marred her skin, evidence of the lightning's brutal strike. From the periphery, Aileen watched with a mixture of horror and hope as they tried to treat Maya, then gently transferred her onto a stretcher, and carefully lifted her into the ambulance's sterile interior.

Inside, the paramedics immediately began an I.V. and worked to stabilize her vital signs, bringing a measure of calm to the critical situation before the ambulance departed the school grounds, its flashing lights leading the way towards the nearest hospital in Garrison.

Slowly, the assembled crowd started to disperse just as the school bell rang, marking the end of morning recess. Amid the rising chatter and the rush of students, Aileen, clearly shaken, quietly made her way back to class.

The remainder of her school day passed in a blur, each lesson a monotonous drone, her mind replaying the unsettling scene from moments before. Though physically present, her thoughts of her best friend remained trapped in the recent past, leaving her feeling hollowed out and profoundly weary long before the final bell chimed.

On the bus ride home, the rhythmic drone of the engine did little to soothe the turmoil in Aileen's mind. Her thoughts remained fixated on the disembodied whisper, that voice that had surged into her consciousness with an inexplicable urgency, telling her the simple yet profound command for her to "*stay inside today.*"

It wasn't menacing, not exactly, but undeniably insistent, possessing an almost ethereal quality that bypassed her logical defenses. The more she replayed the moment, the more an unsettling realization solidified: it felt less like a warning and more like an active presence, as if this unseen entity was deliberately protecting her, subtly guiding her away from unseen peril, constantly overseeing her every potential step.

These recent, bewildering events were not just a fleeting memory; they were etched deep within her, an indelible mark that she knew, with an unshakable certainty, she would neither forget nor ever truly comprehend.

That evening was overshadowed by a heavy stillness over the Byrne household, the air still faintly scented with the aromatic spice of the supper they had barely eaten. Aileen, galvanized by a day spent wrestling with unimaginable dread, could no longer sit still. The chaotic image of the morning—the blinding flash, the sharp crack of thunder that had instantly silenced the schoolyard, and the chilling sight of her dear friend Maya being attended to by paramedics—had played on a punishing loop in her fearful mind.

After dinner, her anxiety manifested itself as an unwavering insistence. She didn't merely ask her parents to call the hospital; she pleaded with a desperate, low urgency, pacing the living room floor until the tension became unbearable for them all.

Her mom and dad, equally concerned but perhaps fearing the confirmation of tragedy, finally relented, agreeing that the agonizing uncertainty was worse than the potential bad news.

Her mom took the wall phone receiver, her hand trembling slightly as she punched the number for the Garrison Town Hospital. Everyone's concern was a palpable mirror of Aileen's own distress. After navigating the sterile bureaucracy of switchboards and transfers, they were finally put through to the third-floor nurse's station—Maya's floor.

The voice that answered belonged to the Head Nurse, Ms. Lane, whose tone was a professional, steady anchor in the emotional storm. There was no urgency, only excellent clarity.

Ms. Lane gently confirmed that Maya had, without question, endured a rough time. The initial hours had involved intense stabilization procedures due to the shock and severity of the lightning strike's impact.

However, after a brief, distressing pause while consulting the on-call physician, the nurse delivered the blessed, comforting news. Her voice, now truly a calm reassurance, confirmed that Maya was displaying a remarkable youthful resilience. "She is, perhaps incredibly, on the path to a full recovery," Ms. Lane stated, the words washing a tidal wave of relief over Aileen, who had slumped into a nearby chair, tears finally starting to fall—but tears of joy.

The final, glorious detail cemented the future: Maya was expected to be discharged and would be returning home in a few short days, needing only brief follow-up care and rest. The entire family expelled a breath they hadn't realized they were holding, the day's crushing fear having been instantly lifted by a simple, life-affirming telephone call.

Aileen was happy to know that her friend would be alright, albeit with a few lasting scars on her arm and shoulder. With a breath of gratitude, Aileen closed her eyes, offering a silent prayer of thanks to God for sparing her good friend from what could have been an unimaginable tragedy.

Aileen went to bed early that night. Despite the alarming events of the day, confidence settled within her, rooted firmly in the belief that her dear friend Maya's recovery from today's unsettling trauma would be not only relatively swift but complete. She pictured her cheerful spirit, knowing that whatever ordeal she had faced, it was merely a temporary shadow, soon to be dispelled by the strength of her inherent ability to bounce back. She closed her eyes and vividly pictured Maya's essence: the fierce, defiant sparkle in her eyes, the quick, sharp wit, the remarkable, sometimes stubborn, refusal to submit to adversity.

5

On the Waterfront

School finally ended for the year, and the summer sun painted the cloudless sky a brilliant blue, a gentle sea breeze carrying the fresh, salty scent of the nearby ocean.

Aileen, looking out the kitchen window, and restless with a burgeoning energy that mirrored the vibrant day outside, felt a familiar tug – the irresistible call of the sea. She turned from the sun-drenched pane to her mother, who was carefully polishing a ceramic mixing bowl. Aileen's eyes, bright as freshly washed sea glass, held a familiar, hopeful glint.

"Mom," she began in a voice that was a little breathy with anticipation, "would it be okay if I went down to the harbor this afternoon? Just for a little while? To see if anything's happening?" She didn't have to specify what 'anything' might be; her mother knew it meant the whole glorious, unpredictable tableau of fishing boats unloading their catch, tourists browsing market stalls, gulls wheeling overhead, and the constant, fascinating ebb and flow of maritime life.

Her mom, a woman who understood the magnetic charm of both the sea and her daughter's spirit, paused her task, a knowing, gentle smile creasing the corners of her eyes. She had seen that particular sparkle in Aileen's gaze countless times before, recognizing the same wanderlust she herself had felt in her youth. "Fine, dear," she confirmed, her voice soft but firm with caution. "Just be careful with the crowds and the working boats, alright? Don't get too close to the edge."

Aileen's "Thank you!" was a joyful explosion in the quiet kitchen. With a swift, she darted to the fridge, grabbing her scuffed, ocean-blue reusable water bottle. It disappeared into the main compartment of her small, well-loved canvas backpack – a repository of dreams and small treasures from past adventures.

As the strap settled comfortably on her shoulder, her mind was already a whirlwind of impending sights and sounds: the distant cries of gulls, the sharp, exhilarating scent of brine and diesel, the rhythmic clatter of fishing nets being mended, the deep horn of an incoming ferry, and the vibrant, unpredictable pulse of life by the water's edge, where every visit promised a new discovery.

Aileen emerged from her house, her gaze immediately falling upon her trusty 10-speed bike leaning patiently against the garage wall. With a cheerful smile and energy, she grabbed it, swung a leg over, and with a slight push-off, was pedaling smoothly east down Main Street. The familiar hum of the tires on the asphalt was a comforting sound. As the vibrant red awning of the corner drugstore came into view, she instinctively peered through the large glass window. Her eyes quickly found their target: Maya, her best friend, stood just inside the front door, engrossed in scanning a magazine, flipping the pages.

Aileen's momentum slowed, her feet straddling the bike as she hovered, waiting. Almost as if on cue, Maya, catching a flicker of movement in her peripheral vision, looked up. A wide smile spread across her face as she spotted Aileen outside, and she lifted a hand in a warm wave.

With an expansive gesture, Aileen made a sweeping motion with her hand toward Ocean Avenue and the sun-drenched harbor beyond, the sparkling water and bobbing boats an unspoken invitation to adventure.

Her hopeful gaze shifted back to Maya, clearly asking if she wanted to come along. Maya, however, merely shook her head from side to side, her lips forming the muted words, "Waiting for mom!" Without breaking eye contact, she then pointed a thumb over her shoulder toward the bustling back of the shop where the register was located, a final, resigned shrug of her shoulders communicating both her desire to join and her unshakable commitment to her current post. "Some other time," she said, silently.

Aileen now headed south down Ocean Avenue, her bike gliding along smoothly as she made her way in the direction of the harbor, riding by the local lobster house,

Harbor's Edge. The salty air grew heavier, a clear sign she was nearing her destination. Finally, the expansive sight of the big wharf at the end of Ocean Avenue came into view. She gracefully dismounted her bike, the hum of the traffic fading into the sounds of the bustling port.

From her handlebars, she unwrapped the small lock and cable and secured the bike firmly to a sturdy, weather-beaten, nearby telephone pole, ensuring it would be right where she left it when she returned.

The pleasant sense of discovery guided her through a few shore-front shops, where colorful trinkets and the scent of salt mixed with faint perfume hung in the air. The steady thumping of her steps carried her along the sun-dappled promenade for a good while, now.

A comfortable weariness began to settle in her limbs, prompting a search for respite. Her eyes alighted on an empty bench, perfectly positioned, and with a soft sigh of contentment, she finally took a seat and took a quick swig of water from the bottle she brought from home.

Before her, the quiet harbor unfolded like a living painting: masts swayed gently, sunlight glinted off bobbing fishing boats and trawlers. But it was the vast expanse beyond the breakwater that truly captured her awe – the deep, endless blue of the ocean stretching to meet the horizon, dotted by distant, almost invisible sailboats and other sea-bound vessels, promising a tempting grandeur far beyond the shore.

The bracing, salt-laced breeze, which usually served as Aileen's natural tonic whenever she was at the water's edge, scrubbing away the week's mental debris and filling her lungs with invigorating purpose, today felt different. Instead of a cleanse, it carried an abnormal chill that raised goose flesh along her arms, a prickle of unease that danced not just on her skin but deep within her marrow.

Then came that stubborn whisper, barely a sound, a spectral sibilant breath not quite caught by her ears, yet chillingly distinct above the raucous, persistent cries of the gulls wheeling overhead - '*He needs help.*'

It sent an icy jolt down her spine, an electric premonition that settled like something dropped in her stomach, a grim foreboding of calamity hanging heavy in the air around her.

Aileen got up from the bench and stepped along the weathered timbers of the old pier, which groaned faintly under the ceaseless assault of the ocean swells. Nearing the end of the main wharf, her gaze was snagged on a scene of disaster.

There, on one of the side docks projecting from the main pier, a small, battered trawler, its paint peeling and rust streaks weeping down its hull, was listing at an alarming angle, its bow dipping precariously into the choppy, slate-gray water. On its slick, spray-lashed deck, a single, desperate figure - a grizzled fisherman in heavy oilskins - struggled with a monstrous, sodden net. The diamond mesh, a hungry maw of ropes and floats, was snarled viciously around one of his legs, and with each surge of the tide, it threatened to wrench him from the precarious footing and plunge him into the churning, frigid depths below. His grunts of effort were now audible even from Aileen's distance, raw with a terror that clawed at her own throat.

Aileen didn't hesitate; a jolt of pure adrenaline shot through her, eclipsing her pervasive dread and propelling her forward. Her sneakers hammered a staccato rhythm on the weather-beaten planks, her focus narrowed on the desperate scene. The cryptic, formless warning, which had initially been a mere prickle of unease, now rang like a chilling gong in her mind, a stark counterpoint to the chaotic splashing and straining grunts emanating from the trawler.

Yet, her fear was momentarily eclipsed by an urgent, primal need to intervene, to fight against the unseen force that seemed to be pulling the man under. Scanning the surrounding proximity, she saw no one remotely close by to assist. She raced towards the chaos with her mind already calculating the quickest way to reach him, every muscle tensed, ready to offer whatever aid she could against the relentless pull of the sea.

The chilling sight sent a jolt through Aileen as she approached the salt-stained fishing trawler, which was rocking precariously in the choppy swells. "Help!" a raw, guttural cry tore through the sea air, belonging to the burly, weathered fisherman who was clinging desperately to the gunwale of his boat and his face was a mask of gaunt terror.

With a trembling, urgent finger, he jabbed towards a heavy, well-honed blade, its steel shimmering menacingly in the sunlight, that was securely mounted in a wooden sheath by the stern. "Cut the line!" he bellowed, his voice ragged with desperation, his eyes wide with an almost primal fear. He pointed down towards his feet, which were obscured by a mass of dark, verdant green nylon netting. "Here! It's got me!"

Without a second's hesitation, Aileen launched herself from the dock, landing with amazing agility onto the pitching deck of the trawler.

Adrenaline surged through her veins, sharpening her focus. She immediately sought out the problem: the thick, multi-stranded fishing net was wrapped mercilessly tight around the fisherman's ankle, the lines biting deeply into his flesh, threatening to pull him overboard with every roll of the boat.

His leg was contorted at an unnatural angle, the ankle bone threatening to snap under the immense, constricting pressure. She lunged for the knife, her fingers closing around the worn, yet surprisingly sticky, cork handle. The heavy blade felt cold and solid in her hand, a tool of grim necessity.

Drawing on every ounce of strength she possessed, every muscle tensing with focused determination, Aileen brought the knife down in a powerful, decisive arc. With one swift, downward motion, a clean, audible *snap* could be heard across the water as the razor-sharp edge slashed through the offending netting. The tension in the lines immediately released, and the severed strands, now mere green rope fragments, fell into a heap at his feet with a liberating thud. A gasp of pure relief escaped the fisherman's lips as he finally pulled his freed, though bruised and scarlet-marked, ankle from the tangle. For a moment, there was only the sound of the seagulls, the creak of the boat, and the shared, stunned silence of a life snatched back from the brink.

The fisherman slowly, almost tentatively at first, then with increasing certainty, extended his hand towards Aileen. It was a hand that told a story: knuckles like gnarled roots, and skin that felt like sun-baked leather – an evidence of a life spent battling the unpredictable whims of the sea. "Thank you, my dear. You saved me!" His voice, though raspy from exertion and shock, held sincerity that transcended mere words, a raw whisper of gratitude for the life he'd almost lost.

Before Aileen could fully process the depth of his emotion, he reached out and, with a grip surprisingly firm despite his evident exhaustion, enveloped both of her smaller, much softer hands within his own. He looked directly into her innocent eyes, reflecting a mixture of awe and overwhelming relief. "You saved my life," he declared, the words not a simple statement but gratitude toward the miracle she had just performed. "What's your name, young lady?" "Aileen Byrne," she responded with a smile. He tightened his hold, "I'm John Wilson. Thank you, Aileen!"

Then, as if to anchor himself to her, to the very person who had pulled him back from a very possible fatal end, asked, "How can I ever repay you for your quick response and bravery, Aileen?", his voice thick with a genuine, almost desperate need to express the unfathomable debt he now owed her, his very being seeming to radiate the depth of his indebtedness.

"No, truly, sir, there's no need for any reward," Aileen replied, in her usually soft voice. She met his grateful, still-somewhat-shocked eyes with a calm earnestness. "I'm just glad that I happened to hear you... and that I was at the right place at the right time to help." Her eyes, sharp and intelligent, swept over the chaos of his deck – the snapped lines, the scuppered water, the diffusing scent of danger and salt.

Then her tone shifted, a gentle, almost maternal admonition entering her voice. "You be careful out there, though, OK? The sea can turn on you in an instant, and it was a near thing just now." Her brow furrowed with genuine concern. "I'm sure your family, wherever they are, wants you back in one piece, whole and hearty, OK?"

With a final, meaningful nod, Aileen turned away. She stepped off the rocking of the boat beneath her feet with grace onto the sturdy, barnacle-flecked planks of the finger pier. Her sneakers made a soft thud as she began to walk, her long stride purposeful as she headed away from the bobbing fishing vessels and toward the bustling heart of the harbor.

But after only a few steps, an impulse made her pause. She stopped, the sounds of gulls crying and distant ship horns seeming to fade for a moment. She glanced over her shoulder, her eyes seeking out the fisherman's boat in the afternoon light. He was still standing there, watching her depart, a hand still pressed to his chest as if to steady a wildly beating heart. Aileen raised her arm slowly and gave a simple, open-palmed wave.

A beat later, he lifted his hand, a jerky, almost awestruck return of the gesture, then offered a slight, wobbly nod of thanks. Seeing his acknowledgment, Aileen turned back, a ghost of a smile touching her lips. The fisherman, with a deep sigh that seemed to carry the weight of his recent terror, finally turned his attention to the laborious task of cleaning up the chaotic mess of scales, blood, splintered wood, and tangled lines on his deck.

Walking on, Aileen's smile broadened into deep satisfaction. The obscure voice, she mused, thinking of that inexplicable nudge, the subtle whisper, the mysterious pull that had drawn her to this very spot, it came through for her, and more importantly, it came through for the fisherman.

It was a quiet triumph, a confirmation of something strange she couldn't quite name, an unseen hand guiding fate's intricate threads. And in that moment, under the vast, indifferent sky, she felt true peace.

Once she got back to her bike, a sense of relief washed over her, even as her hands trembled slightly while she unlocked it from the sturdy pole. With a final glance back at the rolling docks, she pedaled homeward, the chilling events replaying in her mind.

Bursting through the front door, she immediately sought out her family, her voice still a little shaky as she related the harrowing story of what had occurred on the docks, the danger she'd faced, and the quick thinking that had helped her rescue the fisherman. Her father, his eyes wide with a mix of fear and admiration, pulled her into a hearty, reassuring hug, telling her just how incredibly proud he was of her courage.

6

The Encounter

With mid-August upon them, a bittersweet excitement filled the air for Aileen and her friends, as the start of high school loomed just days away, signaling the fast-fading end of their carefree summer. Eager to squeeze every last drop of adventure from their remaining freedom, Aileen, after an early lunch, seized the initiative and called her friend, Maya, suggesting they explore the old trail winding southwest across from her house.

A quick consultation with her mother—who readily agreed with a simple "Just be back for supper, OK?"—secured her participation in the adventure. Maya relayed the good news to Aileen, promising to run right over in a bit, as her home was not too far away from hers, and with that, their final summer expedition was set to begin.

Aileen

With a mix of excitement and nostalgia, Aileen and Maya cautiously walked across busy Main Street, jumped over a small roadside ditch, and stepped onto the overgrown trail, the dirt yielding beneath their sneakers as they delved into the woods a negligible distance across the road from Aileen's family home.

It had been years since their youthful explorations here, but the late summer air still carried whispers of adventure as they navigated the meandering path. The trees loomed overhead, their branches tangling together in a lacework canopy, filtering the sunlight into dappled patterns on the forest floor. Hills and small valleys rose and fell before them, a terrain that seemed both familiar and fresh in the light of their rekindled curiosity.

As the friends wandered deeper into the woods, the sounds of the outside world faded, replaced by an ethereal hush punctuated only by the rustle of leaves and the distant call of a bird or the hoot from a faraway owl.

The well-worn foot trail, which had been their steadfast companion for a mile or so, abruptly dissolved at the lip of a yawning chasm. Below them, the ravine plunged into shadowy depths, its jagged edges hinting at ancient geological forces. Now, to continue their trek, the two girls faced a daunting challenge: bridging this formidable natural barrier. They had two starkly contrasting options, each fraught with its unique challenges.

The first was to attempt a perilous descent down the ravine's sheer, crumbling walls, then face an equally arduous and treacherous climb back up the other side. Glimpsing down, they saw loose rocks and gravel, and precarious handholds that promised a high risk of dislodging boulders or losing their footing, a gamble they were loath to take.

Their alternative, and arguably the lesser of two evils, lay stretched precariously across the gaping void like a desperate, arboreal bridge. It was the immense, gnarled trunk of an ancient pine, shorn of most of its branches, which had fallen with surgical precision between both sides of the open rift.

Its bark, slick with recent dew and moss, offered uncertain purchase, and peering down through the remaining gaps in its branches, they could only guess at the dizzying, rock-strewn depth of the chasm below. A shiver traced its way down Aileen's spine as she eyed the massive log, expressing raw, untamed power. "Perhaps," Maya quipped, her voice a little too light, "that tree was knocked down during the Great Atlantic Hurricane that pounded the southern mid-coast of Maine a few years ago. It certainly looks like it was ripped straight out of the earth."

That infamous storm, still a raw memory for many coastal residents, had indeed been a force of biblical proportions. It's howling winds, clocking well over 85 miles per hour, had not merely 'downed' trees but had ripped ancient oaks and pines, like this one, clean from the earth, their root systems exposed like monstrous claws.

Coastal communities, from the beautiful villages of Boothbay Harbor to the historic port of Kennebunkport, had borne the brunt of its fury. Seawater had surged inland, transforming quaint, cobbled streets into churning rivers, submerging basements, and inundating shop fronts.

Docks, once bustling with boats and pleasure craft, had been splintered into kindling or torn from their pilings, left as twisted wreckage scattered along the shoreline. Fishing vessels, some substantial and unwisely left on their moorings despite warnings, had been smashed against breakwaters, swamped by mountainous waves, or sent sinking to the harbor floor, a sobering evidence of the storm's unbridled power. The very air had vibrated with the sustained roar of wind and crashing surf, leaving behind a landscape scarred by debris and a collective memory of overwhelming devastation that echoed in Maya's casual remark.

The ancient, gnarled pine, felled years ago, lay like a colossal, moss-slicked spine across the gaping chasm. Below, the unseen depths of the ravine seemed to exhale a damp, chilling breath, the distant gurgle of water a constant, unnerving hum in the background.

As Aileen and Maya began their treacherous traverse, each careful step a perilous negotiation with the slick bark and protruding knots, their fingers white-knuckled around any sturdy, available branch, fear was a tangible presence. The air smelled of damp earth and old leaves, and every little creak from the fallen twigs and branches being crushed under their feet seemed way louder than it should've been in the terrifying silence.

It was then, just as Aileen's foot slipped precariously on a particularly treacherous patch, that she again felt it, heard it once more – a faint, icy tendril of a whisper, not inside her head, nor entirely outside, but a chilling presence brushing against her ear. It was that now-familiar, disembodied voice that had made its presence known whenever needed. This time, its message was terse, urgent, and laced with an almost imperceptible warning: *'Be careful! Don't look down.'*

A jolt, cold and sharp, shot through Aileen. Her heart hammered against her ribs, a frantic drumbeat against the silence. Without conscious thought, driven by an instinct far older than reason, her voice, raw with an urgency that startled even herself, tore through the tense air. "Keep looking forward, Maya!" she half-shouted, half-pleaded, her eyes fixed on the distant bank, unwilling to let her gaze waver for even a second. "And watch your step! Don't look down, no matter what!" Maya, startled by Aileen's sudden vehemence, shot back at her a brief, bewildered glance but complied, her face tightening with renewed concentration.

The crossing was like a crawl through molasses where every second felt like a minute, and minutes bled into what seemed like hours. Each carefully placed foot, each trembling grip on a splintered branch, was a small victory against the looming emptiness below.

The air grew heavier, the silence more suffocating, broken only by their ragged breaths and the ominous creak of the old tree. Their muscles screamed, their foreheads beaded with sweat that had nothing to do with exertion and everything to do with terror.

Finally, miraculously, the distant bank came closer, growing into concrete reality. With a collective, unspoken sigh of profound relief, the two girls took their last, teetering steps back onto the solid ground. They didn't just walk off; they practically tumbled, jumping off the precarious makeshift bridge onto the blessed solidity of the earth.

Their legs, trembling like newborn fawns, threatened to buckle, but they remained standing, sagging against each other for a moment, chests heaving, gulping down the sweet, clean taste of air that wasn't laden with fear. The ordeal had been merely minutes, yet it had etched itself onto their psyches with the permanence of hours.

After catching their breath, leaning against a rough-barked tree until the faint tremors subsided, they exchanged a look of shared, unspoken horror and, without a word, continued on their way.

Once the threat had passed, Maya turned to Aileen with an intense look on her face, asking if she wanted to know a secret. After Aileen's intrigued "What's you got?", she slowly revealed a shocking truth: she believed she had died momentarily after being struck by lightning back in April, a confession she had never made to anyone.

Completely spellbound, Aileen instantly stopped Maya on the trail, grabbing her sleeve and demanding to know, "Why? What happened?" Maya recounted how, while swinging high on the very swing Aileen liked, the thunderbolt had struck the metal frame, knocking her to the ground with a thud; but more remarkably, she described seeing herself lying there as a crowd gathered, while *she* stood separate, unseen, looking down at her own body.

A visibly bothered Aileen acknowledged the terrifying nature of the ordeal, and Maya concluded by stating that she was back in her body by the time the ambulance arrived. Peering earnestly at Aileen, she pleaded for her silence, a vow Aileen readily made and kept, promising never to repeat the astonishing tale.

As they continued down the wandering trail, Aileen's thoughts drifted back to that day, to the persistent echo of a voice—a suggestive breath, a soft, insistent murmur that had intricately curled around her youthful resolve, firmly keeping her indoors rather than allowing her to join the boisterous clamor of the playground.

It had been an undeniable premonition then, a quiet caution, and now, with a shiver tracing down her spine, she realized that utterance had been nothing short of a guardian, a silent sentinel shielding her from whatever unseen trouble had awaited the others outside. Aileen wondered if that very presence, an intangible force of protection, was also what had prompted Ms. Davidson to request her to stay behind and help clean the whiteboard, inadvertently keeping her safe once more.

Suddenly, a faint crack, like a tree branch giving way, echoed from farther up the trail, prompting the girls to halt and listen intently. Maya started to speak, but Aileen's urgent "Shh..." cut her off, her index finger pressed to her lips. Peering past the distant curve in the path, they made out a shadowy figure drawing closer from the west. A prickle of unease ran through them as they stood motionless, their eyes fixed on the approaching shape.

What had at first seemed like a spooky illusion resolved into a young, slim teenage boy, perhaps fourteen or fifteen, emerging from the deep shadows. Dressed simply in a t-shirt and jeans, he gripped a well-worn walking stick and carried a small blue backpack. He walked directly up to them, stopped, and offered a disarming smile.

He said, "Hi there! I'm Michael Brown. I'm heading for Applewood. Are you girls going somewhere interesting, or just enjoying the summer day strolling through the woods?"

Maya answered first, "We're just out for some exercise and exploration." Introducing themselves, she said, "I'm Maya, and this is Aileen."

Michael replied, pointing forward to the trail behind the girls, "Good afternoon, ladies! I'm hiking up to Applewood to meet with my uncle, Paul, on his sailboat." He then explained how his uncle had invited him to accompany him as an extra hand on board to navigate his 30-foot cruising sailboat, which he had recently bought, down to Portland, where it would be brought ashore for some repairs and then eventually placed into winter storage.

Aileen, who had been idly kicking at a loose stone, suddenly became acutely aware of him. Her gaze snagged on his easy, confident stance, the way his dark hair caught the sliver of light, and the focused intensity in his eyes.

An immediate, almost visceral "shine" took hold of her, a jolt of something unexpected and warm. A small, involuntary gasp escaped her lips, and a faint, rosy flush crept up her neck and cheeks, betraying the sudden flutter in her chest. A genuine, shy smile blossomed on her face, her eyes brightening perceptibly. Her hand, acting almost on its own accord, lifted in a small, hesitant wave. "Hi, Michael." she murmured, her voice, usually clear as a mountain spring, holding a soft, almost breathy quality as he passed.

Michael offered a quick, easy grin in return, a flash of white against his sun-kissed skin, before continuing his journey. He followed the winding, root-snarled trail that promised to lead eventually to the bustling docks of Applewood harbor, a good hour's trek from their current position. The frequent crunch of his boots on the fallen leaves and twigs slowly faded as he moved further down the path.

Aileen and Maya, who hadn't quite caught the intimate nature of the exchange, watched him trudge steadily away, his silhouette growing smaller with each deliberate step. But as he neared the next sharp curve, where the path dipped precipitously, a sudden, insistent flutter of unease seized Aileen. Her brow furrowed; she remembered the treacherous stretch of trail just beyond that bend.

"Be careful, Michael!" she shouted, her voice cutting through the filtering sunlight with an unexpected urgency. The sound echoed briefly among the woodland. "There's an old tree that fell across the ravine up ahead! It's really slippery underfoot, especially where it's mossy!"

Michael, already halfway around the bend, paused. He turned, a hint of surprise on his face, but quickly registered her concern. A warm smile crossed his lips, and he brought his hand up, giving the old, familiar thumbs-up gesture – a silent acknowledgment, a promise of caution. With a final, reassuring nod, he rounded the corner and was swallowed by the verdant depths of the forest, the sounds of his passage now completely gone.

As the last rustle of leaves died away, Aileen felt a strange, chilling sensation. It wasn't with her ears, not truly, but in the marrow of her bones, a whisper against the very fabric of her soul, that she sensed an almost unheard voice utter, '*Remember him, Aileen. He's a good one.*' It was ancient, resonant, yet barely there, as if woven into the very air of the woods, a secret meant only for her. Her breath hitched, and a shiver traced its way down her spine, though the afternoon was still warm. Aileen gave a small, almost imperceptible shrug, as if to dislodge the memory of the spectral words, a question mark hanging in the air of her mind. *What did it mean? Who had spoken?*

The spectral echo that shimmered just behind her ear struck Aileen with an uncanny familiarity, instantly triggering memories of those previous impossible rescues and strange warnings. It was the same dry, urgent whisper that had warned her away from the terrible accident, and the precise cadence that had later directed her to stay inside that day in school. She realized, with a chilling blend of apprehension and dependence, that this voice was not a sporadic hallucination, but a recurring, precise presence, always arriving just as the stakes became fateful.

She shook her head, trying to dismiss this peculiar sensation, and with a shared glance with her friend, they resumed their journey through the woods, the path ahead, once merely a route, now felt imbued with a subtle, shifting significance.

After hiking a few hundred yards more along the winding trail, they emerged into a small clearing set beside a trickling stream, where obvious signs of past habitation immediately caught their eye. In the center, a small, rock-ringed fire pit held several half-burned sticks and small logs, remnants of forgotten campfires. Scattered nearby were rusted, empty, opened food containers, an old blanket full of holes, and an old discarded, dented teapot, all pointing to a hurried or long-abandoned departure.

Aileen paused, her shoe nudging a scattering of river stones arranged in the telltale circle. The air, suffused with the scent of pine and damp earth, seemed to hold a silent story. She turned to Maya, a wry smile playing on her lips, but her eyes held a deeper glint of curiosity. "I wonder who camped here so long ago." she mused aloud. She looked all over the shallow depression in the earth, barely discernible beneath a carpet of fallen leaves and moss. Nearby, a few gnarled branches, split and weathered, lay haphazardly, hinting at a rough, thrown-together lean-to that had long since collapsed back into the forest floor.

Aileen's brow furrowed slightly as she pictured the scene, her creative mind already imagining the possibilities. She contemplated that this secluded clearing, tucked away behind a thick screen of ancient oaks might have offered a temporary room. Perhaps a poor family, ostracized or simply too destitute to face the judgment of their peers, had sought refuge here.

She imagined them arriving under the cloak of twilight, their few possessions bundled tightly, their faces etched with a weary blend of desperation and hope. They would have stayed for a while, she thought, not a holiday trip, but a survival sojourn, carefully hidden from the bustling crowds and prying eyes of the nearby villages, finding a fragile peace, or at least a temporary respite, in the silent embrace of the wild.

Maya, offering no response, shrugged her shoulders and simply said, "Don't know!"

As the afternoon light began to wane, a silent signal for their return, they turned and started to retrace their steps back in the direction from which they had come. It was then, on the far side of an expansive, open meadow, that they noticed a time-worn sign they must have casually passed by, unnoticed, on their trek south.

The weathered way-mark bore faded, scrawled writing, with the words "Main St. 2 Miles" barely visible in faded red paint, accompanied by a ghostly white arrow pointing left, northward, along their intended return route. A very slight, almost imperceptible path traced the edge of the field, disappearing beneath the outstretched, dark branches of the pines and oaks. Remembering vividly the deep ravine and the treacherous tree-bridge they'd navigated earlier, they exchanged a momentary, knowing glance before speaking in perfectly timed unison, "Let's go that way!"

Turning northward, a sense of grim determination settled over the girls as they began the arduous trek along the treeline, their eyes fixed on the distant promise of home. They pushed through what felt like an eternity, navigating densely-wooded areas where the forest floor was thick with undergrowth and the canopy blocked out the sun, each step a struggle.

Just as exhaustion threatened to overwhelm them, the trees finally thinned, and they emerged into a wide, welcome clearing, the sight of vehicle traffic flowing steadily on the main highway on the other side bringing a wave of relief.

With renewed energy, they carefully but quickly walked towards the road, where they then commenced the long, familiar march east along Main Street, vigilantly facing oncoming traffic. Soon, they at last passed the neighborhood fire department sub-station and knew they had finally reached the comforting familiarity of Applewood.

As the soft, golden hour light began to stretch long shadows across the tree-lined street, the familiar silhouette of Aileen's cozy home came into view. She and Maya paused for a moment. A tired but genuine smile touched Maya's lips as she turned to her friend, her arm lifting in a casual but heartfelt wave.

"What an afternoon, huh?" Maya chuckled, her voice carrying a hint of warmth from their adventures. She stretched her shoulders, a pleasant ache radiating through her limbs. "Man, I'm bushed..." Her eyes, though heavy with the day's weariness, sparkled with the memory of laughter and shared secrets. Aileen returned the wave, her own smile reflecting her sentiment.

With a final glance and a promise of a new day tomorrow, Maya turned to her left and stepped away. There, just beyond a cluster of old oak trees whose leaves rustled gently in the evening breeze, lay the narrow, winding gravel road to her home. It was an intimate path, barely wide enough for one car, bordered by wild daisies and tall grass that brushed against her jeans as she walked.

The distinctive crunch of loose stones under her worn sneakers was a sound as familiar and comforting as her own heartbeat. A short distance down this familiar track, nestled among a small grove of pines, her own family's home, a beacon of familiar comfort with its porch light just beginning to glow, stood waiting for her.

Aileen hurried along, the urgency of the day pushing her forward until she reached her own driveway, where she bolted to the side porch. She quickly ascended the steps, unlatched the door, and slipped into the soothing quiet of her home. Her mother's warm inquiry about her afternoon was met with Aileen's cryptic but telling reply: "Adventuresome, eventful, exhausting, and way too long! I'm tired." Her mom nodded, then informed her that dinner was almost ready and urged her to clean up and get some rest. Kicking off her shoes by the door, Aileen made a beeline for the downstairs bathroom, washed her hands, and then entered the living room, collapsing onto the sofa in a heap.

Later, after a satisfying family meal, Aileen, still feeling the day's weight, excused herself and ascended the stairs for a long, thorough shower. Refreshed, she donned her nightgown, and once inside her bedroom, curled up into her bed, offered a brief prayer, and drifted into a deep, well-deserved sleep.

7

High School

The air in Applewood, on the cusp of autumn, shimmered with a golden haze in late August. There was a light aroma of ripening apples mingling with the warmth of summer, even as the cicadas' dwindling chorus hinted at the season's gentle decline. For Aileen, another year older, however, this wasn't merely the end of another summer; it was the eve of a significant personal transition. She stood at the entrance of a school that felt like a new world, a freshman at the Regional High School at last.

This wasn't just a change of address from the familiar, sometimes suffocating routines of middle school, but a long-awaited start to something bigger. The sprawling brick edifice of the school, with its bustling corridors and a cacophony of locker doors, felt surprisingly energizing. She felt nervous but excited, but it was the latter that truly pushed her forward.

While many of her peers loved the social complexity of lunch tables and after-school clubs, Aileen found her stride not in the whirl of new friendships but within the routine she liked in the classroom.

Here, freed from the often generalized curriculum of her younger years, the more focused classes became the place she both enjoyed and pushed herself in. A spark ignited within her during these periods, a deep, almost physical satisfaction that came from delving into subjects with greater depth.

Advanced Biology, where the details of how cells worked finally made sense to her, captivated her. World History, no longer a mere timeline of dates but full of real stories and consequences, power struggles, and cultural evolution, drew her in with an insatiable thirst for understanding. Even the literature seminars, dissecting the layers of meaning and human emotion within classic texts, became a thrilling intellectual exercise.

Aileen wasn't content with surface-level memorization; she craved the 'whys' and 'hows', the underlying principles and philosophical underpinnings. Her hunger for knowledge was not merely academic; it was an innate, driving force. Each new piece of information was a stepping stone, each discussion a deepening of her comprehension.

* * *

The autumnal light, usually a welcome golden wash, felt stifling within the fluorescent glow of Mr. Henderson's physics classroom. It was one such fall afternoon, with the academic year's momentum building steadily, and the rhythmic drone of a lecture was doing very little to hold Aileen's attention. She found herself drifting into a daydream, looking unfocused, idly across the room.

Her eyes eventually landed on the classroom door, a standard-issue design with a small, wire-reinforced glass pane offering a narrow vista of the world beyond. Even before the jarring jingle of the final bell, an unofficial signal of freedom, she noticed the hallway outside was already teeming with life. A bustling river of students flowed past, a din of muffled chatter, scuffing shoes, and the occasional clang of a locker door, all hinting at an earlier dismissal for some higher grades or simply an eagerness for the day to end.

As Aileen's gaze remained fixed on this lively procession, a sudden blur of motion caught her eye. It wasn't just another student; it was a fleetingly familiar apparition, a quick flash of dark hair and a distinctive stride, as it scooted by her classroom door. Her desk was positioned regrettably distant from the entryway, meaning the figure was in her field of vision for barely a microsecond, a fleeting impression of form and movement. Then, as quickly as it had appeared, it was gone, swallowed by the ceaseless current of the hallway.

Aileen blinked, a peculiar tingle, a spark of recognition, igniting in her consciousness. *No, it couldn't be,* she thought to herself, her brow furrowing in concentration. Contemplating that brief, almost subliminal glimpse, a vivid memory resurfaced. *That kind of looked like...* no, *that really looked like...* the boy Maya and she had met on the sun-dappled trail that day in the woods, a unique encounter from a summer long past. His grace and charm, the way he carried himself – it all rushed back. His name was Michael Brown. She wasn't 100 percent positive, but that name came to her mind with surprising ease.

It was that day in the solitude of the forest, the air thick with the scent of damp earth and pine, when that esoteric whisper, neither breeze nor voice, had curled into her ear: *'Remember him, Aileen. He's a good one.'* The words, cryptic and weighted with a meaning she could not then grasp, now landed with the force of a delayed prophecy. Her breath caught as she wondered, with a heart beginning to hammer against her ribs, what it had truly meant, and just why the whisper had so urgently insisted she must not forget.

Her questioning face deepened, a subtle tilt of her head, eyes narrowed in an attempt to pull the ghostly image back into focus. *Could he possibly go to this school, too?* She wondered. She quickly did a mental calculation. He'd been slightly older than them then, meaning he'd easily be a junior or even a senior now, certainly old enough to walk these very halls. The possibility hung right there.

At the next desk, Chloe Huntley had been idly sketching an elaborate doodle in the margins of her physics notes. Noticing the unusual furrow in Aileen's brow and the slightly parted lips of contemplation, Chloe paused her artwork. "What's with that weird look, Aileen?" she whispered with friendly curiosity.

Aileen, still slightly disoriented by the unexpected visual, shook her head slightly. "Oh, nothing really," she replied, her voice a little hushed, "I just saw someone passing by the door who looked very familiar to me, that's all."

Chloe merely offered a noncommittal "Oh! I see..." her gaze already drifting towards the large, round clock hanging above the whiteboard, its muted hum counting down the final precious seconds to dismissal. Unaware of the thoughts running through Aileen's mind, Chloe simply waited, her attention now solely fixed on the promise of freedom soon to come.

One day, weeks later, clear mid-morning light streamed through the classroom windows, highlighting dust floating in the light. The usual classroom noise was abruptly shattered by a jarring, mechanical shriek. **BEEP. BEEP. BEEP.** The fire alarm's relentless, piercing call echoed through the tiled hallways, a sound designed to cut through any distraction.

For a single, suspended second, a hush fell over Aileen's history class, followed by a wave of tense, excited murmurs. This wasn't the scheduled, mundane drill they practiced monthly; the tone felt different, charged with a genuine, unspoken urgency.

Before any confusion could take root, the school's public address system crackled to life. A female voice, bizarrely calm, filled the void left by the alarm. "May I have your attention. This is not a drill. I repeat, this is not a drill. All students and staff are to proceed to their designated evacuation zones immediately and in an orderly manner, please." The command, delivered with such steady authority, galvanized everyone into action.

With an efficiency born of repetition, their teacher, Mr. Jones, swiftly directed the class. "You know the procedure. Leave everything. Single file, now. No pushing." The students rose as one, a river of backpacks abandoned under desks and hanging from chairs, and filed out into the bustling hallway. The scene was one of controlled urgency. Teachers stood like sentinels at their classroom doors, ushering students along, their voices firm but level. "Keep moving." "Watch your step." "Close the door behind you." Each classroom door was pulled shut with a definitive *click*, a critical fire containment procedure everyone remembered.

The mass exodus moved not as a panicked stampede, but as a trained, organized procession, flowing down stairwells and out through the main exit doors, emerging into the bright, cool air of the paved playground. A safe distance from the main school building, classes coalesced into their assigned groups and teachers conducted hushed headcounts.

It was then that a new sound joined the fading echo of the alarm: the distant, undulating wail of sirens. They began as a faint echo on the wind, but swiftly grew in strength and clarity, splitting the autumn air. Within moments, three massive, gleaming red fire engines, their lights casting frantic red and white pulses across the school's windows, roared into the parking lot, followed closely by a black-and-white police car. The trucks braked with a hiss of air brakes, coming to a stop near the school's main entrance. Doors flung open and firefighters, encased in heavy, yellow turnout coats and helmets, dismounted with a purposeful energy. Some immediately donned air packs, the hiss of regulators a sinister counterpoint to the scene.

During all this commotion, the rising tension, and the acrid bite of smoke that clung to the air, Aileen's gaze, filled with a child's mixture of fear and fascination, swept across the chaos of the schoolyard. Her heart pounded in her chest, a drumbeat of anxiety for the building, but also a quiet hope, knowing it was her father's shift. And then, a familiar, reassuring block of bright yellow, outlined by reflective tape, caught her eye.

It was at this precise moment that Aileen, recognized him despite the helmet and the thick, protective gear. The bold, reflective "20" shimmered on his turnout coat. "There's my Dad!" He wasn't inside, battling the blaze directly, but stood instead at the pump controls of one of the massive red fire trucks, his gloved hands meticulously adjusting dials and gauges.

This was his command center, the critical nerve center of the entire operation, where he monitored pressure settings and water flow, ensuring his crew inside had the life-saving resources they needed.

As his team fought with the fire's fury within the school building, his head, topped with a yellow helmet, swiveled slowly, almost instinctively, across the throng of displaced students and anxious teachers. His eyes, momentarily lifting from the crucial task of maintaining the balance of the water lines, scanned the crowded playground. It was a fleeting, parental check, a moment plucked from the intensity of his duty. And then, across the smoke-hazed distance, their gazes locked.

A slight change in his expression softened his face under the helmet. He gave a small tilt of his head – a silent message she understood even through all the noise. *I'm here. I'm okay. You're safe.* Then, just as quickly as it had come, the personal moment vanished. His professional focus snapped back, checking the pump panel and adjusting the pressure like he'd done a hundred times.

Aileen felt a rush of warmth and sudden admiration. A wide, unconscious smile bloomed on her face. It wasn't just "cool" in the childish sense; it was a deep, strong pride that she felt in her chest. Seeing him there, a linchpin in the unfolding drama, calm and competent amidst the chaos, demonstrated a different kind of strength, a quiet heroism. Her dad wasn't just her dad; he was a protector, a vital part of something much bigger, ensuring the safety of everyone around him. And in that moment, she felt immense gratitude and an unshakable belief that everything would be alright because he was there.

An untold number of anxious minutes passed for the students and faculty huddled outside, speculating in worried whispers. Finally, the chief fire officer, identifiable by his distinctive white helmet, emerged. He held a hand-held radio to his ear before approaching the principal and a cluster of anxious administrators. A collective sigh of relief seemed to ripple through the crowd as the principal's tense posture relaxed. The officer explained that the fire had been successfully extinguished.

Fortunately, he related, it had been confined to a small storage closet in the home economics kitchen. The culprit, he said, was a large, overstuffed box of paper napkins that had been stored on a high shelf, its cardboard corner coming into direct and prolonged contact with the intense heat of an old, high-wattage light fixture, until it finally smoldered and ignited.

With the immediate threat neutralized, the fire crew set about ventilating the building. Using long, heavy-duty extension cords from the trucks, they positioned two large, industrial exhaust fans in the open windows of the affected area, their powerful motors roaring to life to pull the acrid, foul-smelling smoke out into the open air.

Meanwhile, another interior crew conducted a secondary search and a quick inspection of the entire building, checking for any closed doors that had been compromised, ensuring the alarm system was still functional, and verifying that emergency fire hoses and extinguishers were undisturbed and accessible. Simultaneously, after the fire was extinguished, a separate fire crew had entered the building, and worked diligently mopping up the excess water from the floor in the effected room and then securing the area for re-entry by staff and students. Finding all protocols correctly followed and the structure secure, they gave the all-clear.

One by one, the firefighters returned to their apparatus, coiling hoses and stowing gear with professional efficiency. Once every piece of equipment was securely latched in place, they mounted the large trucks. The engines rumbled to life, releasing a cloud of distinctively sharp diesel exhaust that diffused in the cool air. With a final wave to the principal, the trucks slowly pulled away from the curb, their sirens silent now, and they departed the school grounds.

Only then were the teachers given the signal. "Okay, everyone, we're heading back in. Single file, please." The students trooped back inside, with the unusual excitement of the event finally fading. As they entered the main hallway, they were met with the faint but unmistakable odor of burnt paper—a scent that would serve as a reminder of the events of that autumn morning. The alarm was indeed real.

That's when it happened: the now familiar whisper returned, not as an external sound, but a voice that felt like it came from inside her thoughts. It was soft as a baby's breath, yet clear as a bell, there for only a moment. Barely audible even to her inner ear, carrying a calm sort of authority, which she had come to associate with moments when things suddenly made sense, offered a direct, simple suggestion: '*Perhaps, Aileen,*' it began, '*you might like to follow your dad's footsteps and be a firefighter.*'

The mention of her father, a man she deeply admired, stirred something strong inside her. She suddenly felt a clear thought hit her. It wasn't a command, but an invitation, a whispered suggestion that unfurled a path she hadn't consciously considered, yet one that felt surprisingly right. Her immediate, unforced thought, a silent exclamation of a revelation, was: *Hmm, why not?*

Why not indeed? Her father's legacy wasn't a burden, but a beacon. She remembered the pride in his eyes, the respect he commanded in their community, the noble purpose that defined his life. The image of him, strong and selfless, rushing into danger to protect others, had always been a source of admiration rather than fear. The sheer courage, the inherent purpose, the undeniable impact of such a calling... it suddenly made perfect sense to her.

And this memory, this startlingly clear whisper and the subsequent internal affirmation, didn't fade. Instead, it became a compass in the often-turbulent sea of adolescent uncertainty. It remained in the back of her mind throughout high school, influencing her choices, coloring her observations, and subtly shaping the nascent contours of her ambition towards a future she was only just beginning to envision, a future where she, too, might stand on the front lines, a protector and a hero, just like her dad.

8

The Decision

Everything around Aileen felt different, filled with a sense of freedom that was both exhilarating and slightly dizzying, a boundless landscape of uncharted possibility stretching out before her. Not merely the passage of time, but the turning of a definitive page, marked by the confluence of significant milestones.

Aileen, freshly eighteen, stood at this turning point. The smooth, cool plastic of her coveted Maine State driver's license, felt like a powerful key in her hand, a tangible symbol of independence she'd yearned for with every fiber of her being.

And then there's her high school diploma, officially tucked away in a commemorative tube in her closet, represented the definitive closing of a significant chapter – years of classroom bells, structured schedules, and external expectations. It was a clear, exhilarating signal for a new beginning, a life she was now fully empowered to sculpt.

No longer confined by the relentless rhythm of school bells dictating her days, nor the subtle indignity of having to beg for rides, the open road now stretched before her like an endless, inviting ribbon. It promised not just destinations, but spontaneous adventures across the wild, rugged beauty of her beloved coastal hometown – the rocky coves, the dense pine forests, the quaint fishing villages – and, delightfully, beyond. The idea of hopping in the car with no plan felt like a real treat.

While the world away from Applewood seemed suddenly within reach, waiting to be explored with an almost urgent pull, Aileen's practical side recognized the need to first settle down. She understood that true freedom was built on a foundation, and before she could truly launch herself into the wider world, she needed to thoughtfully figure out her options, map out her next steps, and plant her own independent roots.

These two milestones marked the end of being a kid and the start of real independence — and she could finally see a future she'd get to shape for herself.

Driven by a fierce need for independence – and perhaps a touch of desperation – Aileen made the audacious decision to abandon the stifling confines of her previous educational life and seek some distraction down on the rugged harbor side.

She had spoken with someone in town that mentioned that they were looking for someone young and energetic to help out. This wasn't easy work; the docks had their own rough atmosphere — creaking boards, yelling gulls, engines in the distance, and the sharp mix of salt and diesel. She actually enjoyed being down there every time she had a visit.

She wasn't looking for a "woman's work" position; she wanted to dive headfirst into the raw, demanding life of a dock hand. Once hired, her days quickly blurred into a relentless cycle of physical labor, often beginning before dawn with the first fishing boats returning. She'd be hauling heavy mooring lines almost as thick as her arm, guiding towering cargo cranes with shouted commands, or meticulously patching torn fishing nets under the glow of a bare bulb.

There were crates of exotic goods to be unloaded, barrels of pungent oil to be rolled into storage, and the constant, laborious work of sweeping and mending the weathered planks of the jetties. No task was too menial, no heavy lift too daunting, and no weather too harsh to deter her from living the experience.

Her hands, once soft, soon became calloused and rough, her muscles aching with a satisfying fatigue by nightfall. The initial skepticism from the hardened sailors and grizzled longshoremen slowly gave way to a grudging respect, as they witnessed her stubborn determination and unexpected strength.

Aileen learned to interpret the language of the sea—the subtle shifts in the tide, the meaning behind a ship's horn, the whispered warnings of an approaching storm. She was no longer just cute little Aileen; she was "the part-time summer dock hand," a vital, if unexpected, part of the bustling, unforgiving, yet strangely liberating world of the harbor.

The relentless summer sun, a persistent, golden haze over the clamoring docks, seemed to tick in slow motion for Aileen. Each sweltering day, her work bled into the next, marked by the rhythmic clang of cargo against steel, the brine-laced scent of the sea mingled with diesel fumes, and the constant, demanding churn of labor. Yet, beneath the sun-baked surface of her routine, Aileen had a growing idea of a better life.

It wasn't merely about escaping the grueling physical toil of the waterfront, though that was a significant draw; it was about purpose, about carving out a future that felt both meaningful and secure, a life where her intelligence and grit could be put to a different, perhaps more meaningful, use.

Central to this evolving dream was the daunting, yet alluring, possibility of becoming a firefighter, just like her dad. She often found herself watching him return home after a shift, weary but radiating pride, his uniform smelling faintly of smoke, a reminder of his courage and community service.

The idea of donning the turnout gear, of rushing into danger to save lives, resonated deeply with a part of her that craved action and responsibility. It was a legacy, a calling that pulsed through the Byrne family's veins, and the thought of continuing it offered a compelling sense of belonging and honor.

However, this powerful aspiration was perpetually tethered to a gnawing, insidious fear: the fear of not living up to her father's formidable legacy. Her dad, Liam Byrne, was a respected firefighter, a man whose bravery was legendary within their close-knit community. What if she weren't as strong, as quick-thinking, as fearless? What if she failed, not just in the eyes of her colleagues, but in her own, and, worst of all, in her dad's? The pressure of expectation, both internal and external, was a crushing weight.

She keenly understood that while life on the docks, with its relentless demands, unpredictable machinery, and the ever-present threat of accidents, could be incredibly stressful and sometimes outright dangerous, the life of a firefighter carried its own distinct and terrifying perils. The docks threatened physical injury; firefighting threatened the ultimate sacrifice. This profound conflict, a tug-of-war between aspiration and apprehension, weighed heavily on her mind, making every decision, every thought about her future, feel incredibly complex.

Amidst this internal turmoil, a different kind of warmth had begun to bloom in Aileen's life: her relationship with Michael Brown

A few days after Aileen had spotted Michael in the hallway, they met face to face in the school parking lot, igniting a journey that would shape their lives in ways they could have never imagined. Their initial encounter blossomed into a beautiful friendship, paving the way for a love story that would become the envy of their peers.

Their bond flourished through shared experiences that defined their teenage years, marked by the tender moments of high school romance – the jittery excitement of school dances, the hushed confessions exchanged under the moonlit sky, and the quiet harmony as they braved the tumultuous waves of adolescence together. Each memory forged a deeper connection between them, anchoring their relationship in a foundation of mutual understanding and unwavering support.

As time moved swiftly, the inevitable transition from carefree youth to responsible adulthood loomed on the horizon. Michael's graduation signaled a shift in their dynamic, as the carefree days of high school love gave way to the realities of adult life.

With a sense of duty and purpose, Michael took his place at the family business, symbolizing the end of one chapter and the promising start of another. Their love story evolved from innocent infatuation to a mature partnership, grounded in commitment and shared aspirations.

In retrospect, Aileen and Michael's journey embodies the beauty of young love evolving into a steadfast companionship. Their story serves as a testament to the life-changing power of shared experiences and the enduring strength of a bond that weathers the storms of life.

As they navigated the delicate balance between past and future, their love remained a beacon of hope and resilience, guiding them through the uncharted waters of adulthood.

Since they had been high school sweethearts, their teenage romance flickered briefly before the demands of post-graduation life pulled them in different directions. But lately, their paths had converged again, and they had been spending an increasing amount of time together.

What started as casual catch-ups over coffee or late-night walks along the moonlit pier had deepened into something greater. They'd shared stories, dreams, and vulnerabilities under the vast summer sky, and an undeniable intimacy had grown between them. He was attentive, kind, and possessed an easygoing humor that often coaxed a rare, unguarded laugh from Aileen. Now, their connection was beautiful; Michael was, without question, her boyfriend. And seeing how serious their relationship had become, a new idea sparked in Aileen's mind.

The time felt right, she decided, to introduce him to her boisterous, loving, and notoriously opinionated Byrne family.

The invitation was extended, and one warm evening, Michael Brown found himself standing on the porch of the Byrne family home, a nervous smile on his face, a bottle of respectable wine clutched in his hand. The initial introductions were a whirlwind of handshakes, hearty greetings, and the rich aromas of her mother's famous shepherd's pie wafting from the kitchen.

The family, a lively collection of her parents, her younger brother Sean, and a couple of aunts and uncles who were also visiting at the time, was immediately welcoming, though Aileen could feel their curious eyes assessing Michael with a keen, protective scrutiny.

Dinner was filled with laughter, stories of the day's events, and, eventually, the inevitable discussion about Aileen's future. Aileen's mother, Faith, ever practical, gently steered the conversation, asking about Aileen's intentions regarding her summer work on the docks, a job Faith had always quietly worried about.

Michael, emboldened by the warm atmosphere and perhaps a glass of wine, expressed his own mild concern, stating, "Honestly, Mrs. Byrne, I don't care for Aileen working so hard on the waterfront. It's tough, dangerous work, and she deserves something steadier, something that doesn't wear her down so much."

His candidness, delivered with genuine affection for Aileen, seemed to positively impact the Byrnes. Her father, usually pensive, nodded slowly, his concern for his daughter evident in his eyes. Faith chimed in immediately, "You're right, Michael. We've said the same thing, haven't we, dear? She needs to find something more suitable for her."

Even Aileen's usually cynical younger brother, Sean, who had always viewed relationships with a jaded eye, found himself nodding in agreement. "Life's decisions," Sean mused aloud with unusual maturity in his voice, "they can be complicated, can't they? Especially when it comes to finding your place." He was genuinely impressed with Michael's clear employment aspirations – a growing career in finance, steady and promising – and his respectful, articulate way of speaking. He saw in Michael a stability that Aileen often lacked, and it eased some of his own unspoken worries about his sister.

As the evening progressed, questions were asked and answered with an easy flow, getting into Michael's background, his hopes, and his intentions towards Aileen. By the end of the night, it was clear: Michael had charmed the entire Byrne clan. Everyone clearly liked him, and

Aileen felt herself relax. The discussion then pivoted to Aileen's next steps. With Michael's point about her need for a "more steady occupation" still on the table, the entire family seized upon the idea.

A flurry of suggestions erupted around the table: "You're so good with people, Aileen, why not do something in customer service, or even administration at a good firm?" one of her aunts suggested. "With your head for numbers, maybe accounting?" her father offered, a hint of practical hope in his voice. "Or what about teaching? You've always been so patient and structured," her mother added, her eyes sparkling with ideas. The room buzzed with possibilities, each an intended potential path away from the docks, offering a glimpse into a future yet unknown.

Once the dinner plates had been cleared, and her younger brother, Sean, along with her aunts and uncles, retired to the living room, Aileen, her hands clasped tightly around a mug of cooling tea, had been wrestling with the words for weeks. She'd felt it, that persistent, almost *audible* whisper of destiny, an omnipresent mysterious voice that wasn't a sound but a conviction, a deep-seated calling that had grown increasingly insistent. Finally, with a deep breath that hitched slightly in her throat, she looked across the worn oak table at her father, Liam.

"Honestly, Dad," she began, her voice much less steadier than she actually felt, "I've thought about this for some time, now, and I've been contemplating maybe following in your footsteps. Maybe becoming a firefighter would be right for me. I'm fit, I'm smart, and I'd like to serve the community."

This wasn't a sudden whim. She'd spent countless nights buried in online forums, studying training manuals, even discreetly shadowing some of the younger recruits at the station during work hours. She'd pushed her body on the docks, tested her endurance, and even memorized fire codes and first aid protocols until they felt like second nature. The idea had solidified into a concrete plan. "I've looked into the Regional Firefighter Academy," she continued, a spark of determined excitement now overriding her initial nervousness. "I could attend this fall. The application deadline is coming up soon."

Liam, who had been listening intently, a slight crease forming between his brows, leaned back in his chair. A long moment passed as he stared at her. His gaze, usually so steady and warm, held a flicker of something complicated – pride, undoubtedly, but also a familiar apprehension. He knew the dangers of the job intimately, the long nights, the searing heat, the emotional toll, the constant dance with mortality. These were the very reasons he'd often steered her gently toward less challenging paths.

"Well, Aileen," he finally said, his voice carrying a subtle tremor of the myriad emotions swirling within him. "That's... that's entirely up to you, dear." He paused, running a hand over his chin, the practical side of his mind kicking in, a way to ground himself. "I heard that the department will, in fact, have a couple of openings in a few months, when some of the seasoned crewmen will be retiring from the service. Pretty good timing, if that's truly what you want to do."

The phrase offered both a tangible possibility and a quiet, almost pleading question in its undertones, a hope that she truly understood the gravity of her choice. Considering she still resided at home with her mom, dad, and Sean, she had a solid home base to study, work out, and rest when the need became apparent.

A few short days later, the contemplation of the preceding days had finally solidified Aileen's plan. The initial doubts, the exhaustion, the fear of the unknown – all had been processed, leaving behind a renewed and unshakable determination. She decided, with a clarity that felt like sunlight breaking through clouds, to press forward with her ambition of becoming a professional firefighter like her dad, a calling she now understood was deeply ingrained in her soul.

Without delay, Aileen scheduled a crucial meeting with Cameron Stevens, the highly respected current chief of the Applewood Fire Department. What began as a formal discussion quickly evolved into a lengthy and candid consultation, stretching well over an hour in his functional but comfortable office.

Chief Stevens, a man known for his astute judgment and commitment to his crew, listened intently as Aileen articulated her aspirations, her understanding of the challenges, and her dedication to serve. He probed her motivations, outlined the rigorous path ahead, and shared insights from his decades of experience, painting a realistic picture of the demands and rewards of the firefighting profession.

When the conversation concluded, a sense of validation washed over Aileen. Chief Stevens, his expression creased with a thoughtful but encouraging smile, gave her his unequivocal 'green light.' He assured her, with the weight of his office behind his words, that obviously, successful completion of the demanding fire academy courses and final exam was paramount.

More than just passing, he stressed, she needed to emerge from the training not only technically proficient but also possessing an intrinsic sense of being truly "well-trained and ready"—physically, mentally, and emotionally—for the immense responsibilities of the job. Should she meet these rigorous standards, he pledged, he would personally ensure she received the unbiased opportunity for an upcoming open position on the prestigious Applewood Fire Department's force, confident in her potential to serve with distinction.

The following morning, with a newfound sense of purpose and a flutter of nerves, Aileen picked up her phone. After a quick search online for the official contact, she dialed the Maine Regional Fire Academy. Her heart pounded a little as the line rang, but she composed herself, ready to make the first official step towards her dream.

A professional, yet friendly, voice answered, and Aileen introduced herself, explaining her desire to enroll in the upcoming training session. She was then connected to an admissions coordinator who efficiently laid out the details. To Aileen's surprise and a rush of exhilaration, she was informed that the Fall training period was not a distant prospect, but would begin in a mere two weeks. It was an incredibly short turnaround, far sooner than she had expected, or even dared to hope.

But the good news didn't stop there. The coordinator continued, her tone hinting at a stroke of unexpected luck, that there happened to be a couple of vacant positions available in the upcoming training session. Due to a last-minute cancellation and a shifting schedule, these coveted spots had suddenly opened up. Aileen's breath hitched as the offer was made: she could take one of them, but only if she was prepared to accept that immediate, whirlwind timeframe. The implied urgency was thrilling, not daunting to her.

Just as the familiar pull of retreat began to assert its comfortable dominance, that ever dependable uncanny voice once again chimed in, cutting through the mental static with crystalline clarity: '*If you really want this, Aileen, go for it!* It wasn't a suggestion, but a command, the echo of her deepest conviction, a fearless self that always knew exactly what she needed, even when her conscious mind was lost in doubt, pushing her once more to seize the moment she truly craved.

Without another moment's hesitation, Aileen's voice, usually calm, held an undeniable tremor of excitement. "Thank you," she practically gushed, the words tumbling out, "that would be absolutely great! I'm more than ready, mentally prepared and physically in great shape, and I am truly, eagerly anticipating the chance to attend!"

Her sincerity and eagerness were understandable through the phone, sealing her commitment to the intense, life-changing journey ahead. The dream was no longer a distant possibility, but a thrilling reality just fourteen days away.

9

Academy

Aileen breathed a significant sigh of relief when her mother, after some pleading and urging from Aileen, finally agreed to the arrangement, granting her permission to borrow the aging but dependable 2nd family car—a vehicle that had been little-used but for short local errands since her father had acquired his own vehicle to travel to and from the fire station for work. This temporary loan by her mom was less a luxury and more a necessity, as the rigorous, intensive scheduling of the academy sessions often demanded early arrivals and late departures that public transit simply could not reliably accommodate since the academy was about an hour away.

With the keys secured for the duration of the course, Aileen now possessed the reliable transportation she needed, allowing her to focus entirely on her training and studies without the looming stress of calculating travel times or fear of missing a crucial class.

And finally, the crisp autumn air held a familiar scent of wood smoke and anticipation as Aileen at long last stepped through the gates of the Regional Fire Academy with nervous but excited anticipation. It was the culmination of countless hours of physical training and consistent determination, a dream solidified as she officially enrolled in the highly competitive fall fire academy class.

Her days became a relentless gauntlet of education and action. She absorbed the complex firefighting theory, detailing the chemistry of combustion, fire behavior, and strategic incident command planning. Hours were spent wrestling with heavy, uncharged fire hoses, mastering coupling techniques, advancing lines through simulated infernos, and controlling powerful water streams with precision.

She learned correct ladder operations, hefting cumbersome extensions skyward, executing swift and stable raises, and climbing to dizzying heights with tools strapped to her gear.

Building construction became a critical study, understanding structural integrity, potential collapse points, and the dangers inherent in different materials.

Ventilation wasn't just cutting holes, but a calculated art of air flow management to save lives and property. Extrication drills pushed her to her limits, using the 'Jaws of Life' on mangled vehicles and navigating confined spaces to safely rescue trapped victims.

She honed life-saving skills with basic CPR and first aid. The oppressive weight and claustrophobia of Self-Contained Breathing Apparatus (SCBA) became her second skin, learning to navigate zero-visibility environments with only the hiss of oxygen in each breath for company.

She meticulously practiced the care of firefighting turnout gear, understanding that her protective ensemble was her last line of defense.

Radio protocol drills instilled clear, concise communication, a vital lifeline on any scene. Aileen devoted weeks to mastering the intricate, often seemingly counter-intuitive, official Ten-Code system, utilizing exhaustive flashcard drills and relentless self-quizzing until the numerical lexicon became second nature. Beyond the essential drills and physical conditioning that comprised much of their firefighting education, recruits faced the highly technical and crucial challenge of mastering large apparatus operation.

This specialized training encompassed both the art of driving and the complex science of operating multi-ton fire apparatus, each with its unique demands. Classes explored the specifics of a tanker/pumper combination, teaching students how to manage water flow, pump pressures, and navigate its immense size, while also focusing intently on the precise maneuvering and deployment of a 75-foot ladder truck, a skill requiring exceptional spatial awareness and mechanical aptitude.

And the trainees undertook diligent apparatus maintenance classes, knowing the readiness of their apparatus often meant the difference between life and death.

Beyond the technical skills, Aileen was forced to confront and internalize the brutal physical demands – the exhaustion that seeped into her bones, the searing heat, and the muscle fatigue.

Even more challenging was the mental fortitude required: split-second decision-making under duress, managing chaos, and maintaining composure when every instinct screamed otherwise.

And perhaps most significantly, she began to grasp the emotional weight of the profession – the exposure to human suffering and the responsibility for lives.

From the outset, Aileen detected a current of skepticism among some of her male peers. Subtle glances, hushed whispers, and occasionally, thinly veiled doubt regarding her physical capabilities or emotional resilience cast a shadow on her. While unspoken, the message was clear: she had more to prove than the others, her abilities were under constant, unspoken scrutiny.

The grueling demands of the fire academy, a world of blaring sirens, acrid smoke, and relentless physical trials, became the unlikely crucible for Aileen's most important relationships. She quickly formed deep friendships with some of her classmates, a motley crew bound by shared exhaustion and determination. There was Georgia, whose effervescent spirit and quick wit could defuse even the most tense moments, and Hunter, a quiet giant whose steady presence was supportive. Together, they went through early morning PT, challenging ladder drills, and late-night study sessions, forging a bond that went beyond mere friendship— it was like a family built on trust, mutual respect, and the unspoken promise to always have each other's backs when facing the unknown future.

Yet, not all connections were built on such solidarity. A formidable rivalry quickly blossomed between Aileen and Rocco, a naturally skilled recruit whose undeniable talent was matched only by his potent arrogance and self-importance. Rocco possessed an effortless athleticism and a quick grasp of tactics, often outperforming others with a dismissive smirk.

He saw every challenge as a solo performance, cutting corners when he thought no one was watching and making snide remarks about teamwork. Aileen, driven by a deep-seated commitment to duty and the collective, found his showboating and lack of genuine concern for others' struggles infuriating. Their competitive dynamic ignited a silent tension, pushing both to their limits in every timed evolution and physical assessment, creating a constant undercurrent of contest in the demanding academy environment.

It was in the course of this intense training, specifically during the notoriously disorienting "Pitch Black Maze," a confined, smoke-filled activity designed to simulate a building fire that Aileen experienced one of her most poignant academy moments. Hunter, froze midway through the pitch-dark tunnel, a sudden, primal panic seizing him as the simulated smoke thickened and the claustrophobic walls seemed to close in.

His ragged breathing echoed in the oppressive silence. Aileen, navigating just ahead, sensed his struggle. Or was it the always-present whisper in her ear? Instead of pushing forward, she halted, turning back through the oppressive darkness until her gloved hand found his. Even wearing her SCBA breathing mask, her muffled voice was calm and steady despite the simulated chaos, cut through his terror: "Hunter, focus on my breath. Remember your training. You're not alone. I've got you." Slowly, painstakingly, she guided him, step by hesitant step.

Aileen's oxygen tank alarm was blaring as she and Hunter emerged, breathless but determined, into the fresh air outside. In that critical moment, Aileen didn't just perform her duty; she shattered the others' preconceptions. A newfound, grudging respect replaced the quiet undertones of doubt, a clear acknowledgment of her courage and capability within the intense world of firefighting.

When the pair had finally emerged, gasping for fresh air, Hunter's eyes met hers, not with embarrassment, but with gratitude that solidified their bond into something unbreakable. It was a stark reminder that true strength often lay not in individual prowess, but in the courage to support another when they needed it most.

During her intense and all-consuming time at the Fire Academy, Aileen found herself in a relentless struggle to balance the brutal demands of her training with the rapidly shrinking fragments of her personal life. From dawn till dusk, and often long into the night, her existence revolved around the academy's rigorous schedule. She'd spend her days wrestling heavy hoses, scaling drill towers, navigating smoke-filled training simulations, and enduring grueling physical conditioning that left her muscles aching and her hands calloused.

Every evening, instead of unwinding, she'd return to her small upstairs bedroom, which had been transformed into a sterile study zone, littered with thick manuals outlining emergency protocols, fluid dynamics, and hazardous material classifications. The whirring of the ventilation fan in her room often accompanied the rustle of turning pages long after midnight, as she carefully memorized every knot, every piece of equipment, and every life-saving procedure required by the demanding firefighting curriculum.

Consequently, her social calendar, once vibrant with weekend outings and movie nights, had evaporated. Michael, her longtime boyfriend, who himself navigated the ruthless, high-stakes currents of the finance world, understood the demands of ambition. Yet, a quiet frustration began to fester beneath his unquestionable support.

He frequently found himself eating dinner alone at his apartment, his calls and texts often going unanswered for hours, or receiving short, exhausted replies. While he was diligently building his own career, often working late himself, he still carved out time for Aileen – time that increasingly went unfulfilled. He deeply admired her dedication and supported her dream with every fiber of his being, but the constant absence and her distraction when they *were* together started to wear on him.

Even her dad, Liam, a man of observation, couldn't ignore the shift. One Sunday, as the family gathered for their traditional dinner – a rare occasion without Aileen – he remarked with a soft sigh to his wife, Faith, "It's been weeks since Aileen joined us for a proper meal. I know she's chasing her dream, but it seems she hardly has time for dinner with the family anymore."

His words, though not accusatory, were a subtle reminder of the sacrifices Aileen was making, not just for her future, but in the present, deeply impacting those who loved her most. The dream of becoming a firefighter was consuming her entire world, leaving little room for anything else.

And so, one particularly quiet and lonely evening, after yet another carefully planned date – a quiet dinner, maybe a movie, or just a chance to talk – was unceremoniously rescheduled due to a "mandatory study session," Michael's patience finally wore thin.

A slow, simmering resentment had been building within him, eclipsed only by the ache of neglect and worry for Aileen. He'd tried to be understanding, had genuinely cheered her on through the grueling demands of the Fire Academy, but the constant cancellations, the hurried phone calls, and the noticeable absence of her presence in his life had begun to take their toll.

The drive to Aileen's home felt heavier than usual, the familiar route now felt laced with unvoiced concerns. He parked, the car engine ticking quietly in the still night, and took a fortifying breath. After being let inside by her mom, he said a quick, "Excuse me..." and headed directly for the stairway. The 'storming' upstairs to her bedroom was less an act of raw anger and more an urgent, determined push to finally breach the invisible wall that had grown between them. He found her, as expected, hunched over a stack of manuals and notebooks, the room dimly lit by a study lamp, a half-empty coffee cup beside her.

Aileen glanced up, startled, her eyes wide with surprise and a flash of what looked like guilt. Michael walked over to her, his heart aching at the sight of her tired face. He gently took her hand, his thumb tracing slow circles on her knuckles, and sat on the edge of her bed. "Aileen," he began, his voice a low, resonant rumble, stripped of accusation but full of grief. "I support you, you know that. One hundred percent. I always have, always will."

He paused, gathering his thoughts, careful to choose his words. "But sometimes... sometimes I think you've become overly obsessive. It feels like you're disregarding, well, your family and the rest of your young life. Us. Your friends. Everything outside of the fire academy."

His gaze was tender but serious, his words hanging in the quiet air, weighted with a truth she secretly acknowledged in the long lonely hours, but couldn't yet bring herself to confront, let alone articulate.

Aileen's shoulders sagged, a soft sigh escaped her lips as she finally met his gaze. Her eyes began to cloud with a mixture of weariness and genuine remorse. She admitted that she'd been working diligently, almost punishingly so, to complete the arduous Fire Academy courses. Her voice was small, tinged with a regret that echoed his own feelings of neglect.

"I'm so deeply sorry, Michael," she whispered, her fingers tightening around his. "For neglecting you, and my parents. I really am." She explained how she felt an overwhelming, almost suffocating, need to not just pass, but to excel in the firefighter course – to prove to herself, beyond any doubt, and especially to her father, who had subtly questioned her physical and emotional strength for such a demanding career, that she could handle it. This wasn't just a course; it was a personal affliction she felt compelled to overcome.

She then leaned closer, her expression genuinely earnest. "Michael, dear," she explained, "there's only one more week remaining to complete the course. Just the final, grueling practical assessment to perform, which feels like the culmination of everything, and then it's ending with the written graduation exam." Her voice was laced with both exhaustion and a desperate hope.

She promised, with a fervent intensity Michael knew she would honor, that things would return to normal – their normal of shared laughter, quiet evenings, long talks, and spontaneous adventures – once all this relentless hard work was finally finished.

Before he could respond, she reached over, her hands finding his shoulders, and pulled him in close. Then, with a depth of emotion that spoke volumes, she gave him a long, heartfelt kiss – a kiss that was both an apology and a promise, a reassurance and a desperate plea for his understanding.

Pulling back just slightly, their foreheads still touching, a soft, tired smile bloomed on her face. He returned it instantly with relief. The dense, unspoken tension that had permeated the room and their relationship seemed to just float away, dissipating like smoke into the quiet night.

At that point, the heavy, deliberate stomping of footsteps echoed up the stairs, followed by the sight of her dad pushing open the door, his brow furrowed with concern as he asked, "Everything OK up here?" Aileen turned facing him, offering him a reassuring smile. "Yes, dad," she replied, her voice steadying. "We discussed things, and all will be fine soon..." She then looked back at Michael, softening as she continued, "I promise. I'm truly sorry if I've been distant from everyone lately, but I've been working incredibly hard, and all the pressure will be over very soon."

Michael, now feeling not only deeply relieved but somehow even more intimately connected to Aileen through their shared vulnerability, enveloped her in a comforting hug. He held her tight for a few moments, a silent affirmation of his love and renewed understanding. Dad had gone back downstairs, and Michael left her to continue her studies, the weight in his chest notably lighter, knowing full well that her unwavering determination, now acknowledged and understood, would see her through to graduation and beyond the Fire Academy, into the courageous life she so fiercely desired.

Subsequently, the fateful date arrived. The crisp dawn air, usually a harbinger of calm, crackled with concern on the day of the all-encompassing final practical firefighting tactics assessment. This wasn't merely a test; it was the ultimate proving ground, the culmination of weeks of grueling, relentless training where every hands-on drill had been taught, refined, and practiced repeatedly. All the recruits, stiff with nerves and anticipation, gathered in the staging area, the scent of diesel, wet canvas, and stale smoke clinging to the very air. In order to allow the recruits to rest and recuperate between exercises, they would take his or her turn fulfilling the required exercises one at a time.

Aileen, with her jaw set in determination, was first up for the timed donning of her personal protective equipment

– an immediate and critical benchmark. Her movements, honed by muscle memory, were a blur of noticeable efficiency. The heavy, unyielding turnout boots slipped on, followed by the stiff, fire-resistant pants which she snapped and buttoned shut with a practiced tug. The bulky turnout coat swiftly followed, its collar secured high about her neck, then the protective Nomex fire resistant hood. The metallic clang and hiss of the Self-Contained Breathing Apparatus (SCBA) tank being shouldered was a familiar sound, its weight instantly settling onto her back.

With an expert sweep, the face mask was donned, sealing her in a muffled, fog-prone world, the air supply hissing softly into her ears. Finally, the protective helmet was cinched, its brim obscuring her peripheral vision but offering a vital shield. Every second counted, every movement precise, aiming for the perfect, unhesitating execution that could mean the difference between life and death in a real emergency.

Later, out on the training grounds, came the demanding gauntlet of hose operations. Aileen began with the urgent deployment and large-diameter feeder hose hydrant hook-up, a task requiring both strength and meticulous precision to ensure a robust water supply. With the main line secured, she moved to the fire truck, swiftly removing a charged hand-line, its weight substantial as she dragged it, serpent-like, towards the smoke-filled training facility. This simulated environment, thick with acrid, dark smoke, demanded navigation by touch and instinct, advancing steadily into the unknown, maintaining control of the powerful nozzle, and demonstrating proper search and rescue patterns. Her lungs burned as she then had to carry a coiled 1-1/2 inch attack line, its weight threatening to pull her backward, up three relentless flights of stairs, non-stop – a brutal test of endurance essential for reaching upper floors in taller buildings.

After each trainee had finished this segment, the evaluations shifted to the complex mechanics of pumper truck control, where Aileen had to demonstrate not just knowledge, but strategic thinking under pressure.

This included correct apparatus placement for the intended use at the scene, considering factors like wind direction, access points, and potential hazards. She then had to flawlessly execute various pump functions and complex pressure management, adjusting gauges and levers with a keen understanding of hydraulics to deliver precise water flow.

A critical demonstration was drafting from an open water source – a simulated pond nearby – a vital skill for rural firefighting where hydrants are scarce. The rhythmic thrum of the engine, its powerful roar concentrated into the purposeful suction hose, was the soundtrack to Aileen's practiced expertise. Each surge of water drawn into the gleaming red truck was a testament to her unwavering focus and the hours of training that had honed her instincts. She navigated the hydraulics with an almost intuitive grace, coaxing the raw power of the machine into a precise, controlled torrent. The steady flow, a silvery ribbon connecting the earth to the apparatus, was more than just water; it was a tangible manifestation of her skill, a chorus of exertion that spoke volumes about her command of a complex and vital task.

The grandeur and technicality of the ladder truck phase followed. Aileen, often working in coordination with a partner, was tasked with setting up the towering aerial apparatus. This involved meticulously deploying its hydraulic outriggers and stabilizers to ensure rock-solid stability on uneven terrain. With the base secured, she extended the massive ladder to its full, impressive length at approximately a 45 degree angle. A slow, powerful whine of hydraulics accompanying its ascent. Then, with unwavering focus, she safely climbed the dizzying height to the very top, where she demonstrated correct nozzle functions, adjusting stream patterns from solid to fog, sweeping the stream back and forth, simulating fire attack from an elevated position.

Beyond the aerial, proficiency in ground ladders was also paramount. Aileen had to show seamless skill in raising and lowering a heavy 40-foot aluminum extension ladder, a demanding task requiring perfect synchronization and strength from two individuals. She then tackled the more agile 20-foot wall ladder, displaying its versatility for quicker access. Further demonstrations included the proper deployment and use of a roof ladder, designed for secure footing on sloped surfaces, and the compact folding attic ladder, essential for navigating tight, confined spaces within structures.

Finally, the assessment culminated in the high-stakes rescue portion. Here, Aileen demonstrated the proper hook-up and expert use of various power equipment. The "Jaws of Life" came alive in her hands, its hydraulic scream tearing through simulated vehicle wreckage as she strategically cut and spread metal to extricate a "victim" with both force and delicate precision.

Next, the gas-powered ventilation saw roared to life, its churning blade sending simulated sparks and debris flying as she executed strategic cuts into a mock roof, demonstrating critical ventilation techniques to clear smoke and heat, proving her readiness for the most dangerous and decisive moments on the fire ground.

With the fire ground evaluations ended for her, exhausted but emboldened, Aileen finally stepped away, every fiber of her being humming with the raw energy of accomplishment, having proven herself capable and prepared for the formidable challenges ahead.

10
Exam

After a long, rejuvenating night's sleep in the comfort of her home, Aileen felt a renewed sense of determination as she prepared for what would be the final day of testing at the fire academy. The morning air carried a feel of significance—today wasn't just another day of drills or study sessions; it was the conclusion of all the grueling effort on her part, late-night cramming, and relentless physical training. The Maine Regional Fire Academy had pushed her to her limits, but now, on the precipice of completing the final written exam, she could almost taste the satisfaction of victory. Passing this test would solidify what she already knew in her heart—firefighting wasn't just a career path; it was her calling, her future.

The examination room was expansive, with high ceilings and rows of long tables lined up in precise order, each seat to be occupied by a candidate equally as anxious as she was. Aileen found her designated spot, marked by a small placard with her name printed neatly in bold letters. As she settled into the hard-backed chair, the lingering soreness from yesterday's physical endurance test pulsed faintly in her muscles—a reminder of the obstacles she had already conquered. Yet, despite her confidence, a sliver of unease gnawed at her as she stared down at the testing materials in front of her: a sealed white exam booklet, its edges crisp and untouched, two perfectly sharpened number 2 pencils, lying parallel like soldiers awaiting orders, and one cold bottle of water. The front of the booklet bore an unmistakable warning stamped in thick, authoritative black letters:

"MAINE FIRE ACADEMY FINAL EXAM.

NOT TO BE OPENED UNTIL INSTRUCTED TO!"

The redundancy of the instruction almost made her smirk—who in their right mind would risk opening it early?—but the gravity of the moment quickly sobered her thoughts. This wasn't just any test; this was the final barrier between her and the certification she had sacrificed so much for.

Just as she was steeling herself for the challenge ahead, a sudden eruption of noise from across the room shattered the tense silence. Voices—sharp, angry, and urgent—rose above the low murmur of nervous chatter. Aileen's head snapped toward the source of the commotion, where she saw an instructor looming over one of the tables, his posture rigid with disapproval. Fists slammed against the table's surface in what sounded like a mix of protest and desperation, and then, to her astonishment, a figure was being forcibly escorted out of the room.

Aileen turned to Georgia, her closest friend at the academy, who had just taken the seat beside her. Georgia's brow was furrowed, lips pressed into a knowing frown.

"What the hell was that all about?" Aileen whispered, her eyes still fixed on the now-vacant spot where the disruption had occurred.

Georgia leaned in slightly, keeping her voice low. "I think Rocco just got busted for cheating. He cracked open his exam early—tried peeking at the questions before the official start. One of the instructors saw him and lost it."

A stunned breath escaped Aileen. *"Seriously?"* She knew he had issues, but had never pegged Rocco as the type to risk everything over a moment of desperation, yet here they were.

Georgia shrugged. "Yep. They yanked his packet right out of his hands and told him to hit the road. Permanently."

Aileen exhaled slowly, shaking her head in disbelief. "Well," she muttered under her breath, "guess he asked for it."

She turned back to her own untouched exam. The room had quieted again, with tension thicker than ever. But unlike Rocco, Aileen wasn't there to cut corners. She was there to earn her place—fair and square.

As the older head instructor finally stepped forward at the head of the room, Aileen straightened in her seat, a silent resolve to prove herself once and for all etched on her face. The ever-present guiding whisper reiterated '*You got this!*'

Towering in front of the recruits, the instructor's stern voice cut through the silence, first clarifying the slight disturbance from moments ago, unequivocally reminding them that cheating of any kind would never be tolerated.

He then transitioned, advising, "Turn off your phones, relax, take your time," and assured them that water had been provided for thirst. His gaze sweeping the room, he cautioned, "You have two hours to complete the exam. Once done, please grab your papers and return them to the assistant by the exit door." With a final, resonant, "Good luck! You may now begin!" the air released its breath, and the rustle of papers signaled the start of the test.

Every minute felt like a firebomb as Aileen methodically worked her way through the final exam. The hushed intensity of the examination hall was punctuated only by the soft scratching of pencils and the occasional rustle of paper, with the relentless ticking of the wall clock a subtle, yet omnipresent, reminder of time's swift passage.

A few particularly thorny questions had initially caused her brow to furrow in concentrated frustration, the answers momentarily elusive, feeling as fleeting as mist. Her mind would go blank, a small flicker of panic threatening to ignite, but each time, that quiet, persistent inner voice, and a culmination of countless study hours and lecture recall, began to gently unravel the tangled threads of her memory. It prodded her, not with specific answers, but with pathways – prompting her to recall key concepts, methodologies, and logical frameworks that helped guide her towards what she desperately hoped were the correct solutions.

Finally, with only a few minutes to spare, Aileen wrote her last word, the pencil feeling heavy in her slightly cramped hand. A deep exhale, a release of tension that had coiled in her shoulders for the past 120 minutes, finally escaped. As she reviewed her work one last time, a sense of fragile satisfaction bloomed within her; she had given it her all, and she was, in that moment, pleased with the comprehensive nature of her efforts, even if uncertainty still hovered around the edges.

Her limbs, stiff from prolonged stillness, welcomed the stretch as she rose. The crisp white answer booklet, now filled with the indelible marks of her effort and hopes, felt oddly heavy in her hand. Following the before-exam instructions, she carefully walked towards the exit where a faculty assistant, looking almost as weary as the test-takers, sat at a small table by the door.

With a nod and a soft "Thank you," Aileen handed over her completed exam. The act felt surprisingly momentous, like relinquishing a piece of herself.

Stepping out of the building, satisfied that she had done her best, the mid-morning breeze hit her face, a welcome balm to her slightly flushed cheeks, but it did little to disperse the mental fog. Her mind, an incessant echo chamber, immediately began replaying the trickiest questions, meticulously dissecting her responses. *Did I get that one right, the one about the thermal dynamics theory? What about the fire scene analysis for the second essay prompt?*

A tiny, persistent worm of doubt gnawed at the edges of her emerging relief. She walked, oblivious to her surroundings, mentally flipping through the pages of the exam she'd just completed, trying to reconstruct every answer, every calculated guess. There was nothing more to do, no more notes to consult, no more answers to change. The die was cast. Only time, agonizing days perhaps, would tell the true tale of her performance, the final grade a looming verdict. It was now truly over; all that remained was the agonizing, yet inevitable, period of anticipation.

Late autumn gradually deepened into the undeniable, sharp embrace of early winter. A subtle, persistent chill now permeated the air, painting the breath of anyone outside in frosty plumes and hinting at the snow-laden days to come. It was against this backdrop of encroaching cold that a period of agonizing anticipation was playing out for Aileen.

Approximately seven long, nerve-wracking days had ticked by since her final exams at the academy, each sunrise bringing a renewed, unspoken hope, and each sunset a quiet disappointment. Then, late one afternoon, as the slanting sun cast long shadows across the frost-kissed lawn, the moment finally arrived.

Her younger brother, Sean, a lanky fourteen-year-old with an unruly mop of brown hair, was absorbed in a spirited game of catch with his best friend, Mark, in the front yard of his house. The rhythmic thud of the baseball hitting their worn leather mitts was a familiar soundtrack to the quiet suburban street when the old chug of the mail truck broke the afternoon's tranquility.

Sean paused mid-throw, his eyes tracking the familiar blue and white postal truck as it pulled up to their curb. A jolt of realization shot through him. He knew, with a certainty that only a younger sibling could possess, how desperately Aileen had been waiting. Her anxiety had been almost noticeable these past few days, a silent hum of anticipation that permeated the whole house.

Dropping his mitt and the baseball on the damp grass, Sean jogged towards the weathered black mailbox, his heart already quickening. He pulled open the small door, retrieved the thick stack of contents, and began to meticulously shuffle through the usual assortment: a grocery store flier, a glossy magazine addressed to his dad, a few bills, and the inevitable junk mail. His fingers worked quickly, with a focused intensity in his eyes, searching for *that* specific item.

Then, his breath hitched. Tucked between a bank statement and a roofing ad, there it was: a modest, yellow-colored envelope, slightly thicker than the others, and, most importantly, bearing the distinctive return address of the Maine Regional Fire Academy, with "Aileen Byrne" elegantly printed below. A wide grin split his face. As usual, not bothering to close the mailbox, and without a second thought for the game he'd abandoned, he spun on his heel and sprinted towards the house, his shoes digging into the lawn. Before he even reached the porch, his voice erupted, a triumphant, almost frantic shout that echoed across the quiet neighborhood. "I think it's here! Aileen! I think it's here!"

Upstairs, in her quiet bedroom, Aileen was attempting to distract herself with the mundane task of straightening her dresser drawers, though her mind was miles away, replaying every moment of her grueling academy training. The sudden, piercing shriek from downstairs shattered the stillness. It wasn't just a shout; it was Sean's excited, unrestrained yell, a sound she instantly recognized as bearing immense significance.

A wave of adrenaline surged through her veins. Her heart, which had been beating a slow, steady rhythm of hopeful dread for days, now thrummed with a frantic energy. *It's here,* she thought, a certainty blooming in her chest that transcended mere possibility.

Without hesitation, she rushed to her window, pushing up the sash with a sharp click, letting in a gust of cold air. Leaning out slightly, her voice, though eager, was surprisingly steady as she called down, already knowing the answer, "What's here, Sean? What did you find?"

Below, Sean, now standing at the front door, his face flushed with exertion and excitement, practically bounced on the balls of his feet. He held the envelope aloft like a precious trophy. "An envelope from the Fire Academy, Aileen! It's *the* envelope!"

The words were all the catalyst Aileen needed. The neatly folded clothes she'd been sorting were scattered and forgotten on her bed. In a blur of motion, she launched herself away from the window, her feet barely seeming to touch the floor as she flew down the staircase, her urgency propelled by a whirlwind of hope and, at the same time, fear.

She burst into the entryway just as Sean, still beaming, swung open the door. He extended the slightly crinkled envelope, almost reverently, towards her. Aileen's hand shot out, her fingers trembling slightly as she snatched it from his grasp, the paper feeling almost impossibly light yet significantly heavy in her palm. Her breath hitched. For a moment, she just stared at it, a thousand scenarios flashing through her mind. Then, with painstaking care, she gently tore open the top flap as if the slightest mistake could alter its contents.

She slid the official-looking sheets of paper from within, her eyes devouring the words on the cover sheet as they came into focus. Her gaze raced down the page, past the formal letterhead, past the date, straight to the heart of the message, her lips silently forming the words: "Congratulations, Aileen Byrne, on your successful completion, with honors, from the Maine Regional Fire Academy."

Attached to this opening letter was the actual, official, accredited certificate, printed in red, gold, and black ink on stiff, tan parchment paper. Across the top was an outline of a pumper fire truck. In the lower left corner was the official seal of the Maine Regional Fire Academy. She was mesmerized for a moment and thought to herself, *Wow! It's just beautiful!*

The dam of her composure then burst. A primal, guttural scream of pure, unadulterated joy erupted from Aileen's throat, echoing through the hallway and rattling the pictures on the wall. "I did it! Oh my god, Sean, I actually did it! I'm a full-fledged certified firefighter! Just like Dad! I'm finally a firefighter!" Her voice cracked with emotion, a mix of disbelief, triumph, and sheer elation.

Tears, hot and shimmering, immediately began streaming down her flushed cheeks, blurring her vision as a wide, triumphant smile spread across her face. Sean, equally thrilled for her, closed the distance between them in a step, wrapping his arms around his older sister in a fierce, brotherly hug. He pressed a quick, affectionate kiss to her damp forehead, his voice thick with genuine pride. "Good for you, sis! I knew you could do it! I never had a doubt, honestly!"

Below, in the slightly damp, cinder-block confines of the basement, Mr. Byrne had been meticulously working on repairing a frayed power cord for the old vacuum cleaner at his workbench, the quiet hum of his soldering iron filling the air.

Sean's initial shouts had been a distant murmur, but Aileen's subsequent, ear-splitting scream of triumph was unmistakable. He dropped his tools, placing the soldering iron safely on its holder, his heart instantly swelling with a knowing pride. He didn't need to hear the words; he knew what that sound meant.

Scrambling to his feet, he bounded up the wooden basement steps two at a time, his heavy work boots thudding rhythmically, and his own face already beaming. He found Aileen still clutching the letter and certificate, tears and laughter mingling on her face, Sean's arm still around her.

Without a word, he wrapped them both in a powerful, all-encompassing hug, his voice thick with emotion as he held his daughter close. "I'm so incredibly proud of you, dear. So, so proud. I never had a single doubt in my mind that you would do this." The three of them stood there, entwined in a moment of joy, the silence of the house now filled with the warmth of shared victory and familial love.

The very next day, a sense of electric determination coursing through her veins, Aileen awoke before the first hint of dawn. She barely remembered the restless night, her mind buzzing with Chief Stevens' words, a potent mix of challenge and promise. Without hesitation, she drove directly to the imposing Applewood Central fire station office.

The building itself seemed to breathe history and purpose, a sturdy brick edifice that smelled faintly of polish, and the metallic tang of machinery. Inside the administrative office, which was surprisingly quiet save for the distant, muted hum of the heating system, Aileen approached the secretary at the front desk.

Her heart thrumming with a mix of nerves and purpose, she formally requested the application for the firefighter position. The kind-faced administrative assistant handed her a thick packet, and Aileen, refusing to delay, found an empty chair and small table in the waiting area and began filling out the required forms right on the spot. Each stroke of her pen was deliberate, each box a silent affirmation of her perseverance.

As she meticulously wrote, her thoughts drifted back to Chief Cameron Stevens and the conversation they'd shared. His words resonated with a clarity that cut through any remaining self-doubt: "She needed to emerge from the training not only technically proficient," he had stressed, detailing the mastery of complex protocols, the swift precision of equipment handling, and the encyclopedic knowledge of fire science and rescue techniques, "but also possessing an intrinsic sense of being truly 'well-trained and ready'—physically, mentally, and emotionally—for the job."

This wasn't just about ticking boxes; it was about an inner personal evolution.

Physically, it meant infinite stamina, formidable strength, and the raw power to confront life-threatening situations.

Mentally, it demanded lightning-fast critical thinking, problem-solving under duress, and decisive action in chaos.

And, emotionally, it required steel nerves coupled with empathy, the ability to navigate trauma and grief with an unshakable moral compass. It was about developing a deep-seated resilience, an intuitive understanding of a scene, and an unflinching readiness to face the grimmest realities.

Should she meet these rigorous, all-encompassing standards—which he had made clear during their initial meeting were high—he had pledged, with the gravity of a man whose word was his bond, that he would personally ensure she received the opportunity for an upcoming open firefighter position.

Chief Stevens, a man who saw potential where others might only see inexperience, had conveyed his deep confidence in her as the daughter of Liam Byrne, a well-respected member of the department. He believed implicitly in her capacity to serve with distinction, to become not just a firefighter, but an exemplary guardian of the community.

Aileen understood the enormity of his trust and the magnitude of the journey ahead, recognizing it as a calling far beyond a mere career, a path that demanded nothing less than her complete and utter commitment.

This wasn't merely a job application; it was a test of character, a gateway to a highly coveted role on the prestigious Applewood Fire Department's force, an organization legendary for its rigorous standards and unwavering dedication to public safety.

After precisely verifying every single entry, every date, every signature on the meticulously compiled firefighter application forms, and feeling the satisfying *thud* as she dropped the thick envelope onto the desk of the waiting secretary, Aileen felt an overwhelming wave of accomplishment wash over her as she finally began her journey home. It was as if a physical burden, carried for months, had been unceremoniously released.

The secretary, a kind but businesslike woman, had offered a warm smile, but her words carried a quiet reminder of the reality: "We'll be making our final decisions in the coming weeks, Aileen. We've had a truly exceptional pool of candidates this year for the three positions we currently have open." Aileen nodded, acknowledging the stark odds, but even that knowledge couldn't dampen the deep glow of hope that now enveloped her.

The immense weight of months of meticulous preparation – the physical training, the late-night studying of protocols, the agonizing over every written word – had lifted from her shoulders like a heavy cloak shed in the spring sun. In its place surged a buoyant, almost effervescent energy.

Her mind wasn't just buzzing; it was a vibrant hive of hopeful anticipation, each thought a tiny, excited bee flitting with possibilities for the future that now seemed tantalizingly within reach.

Her imagination, now unrestrained, painted vivid scenes: herself, standing tall and confident in the crisp, dark blue uniform, the badge gleaming, the heavy boots grounding her. More than that, she saw herself as a vital part of a cohesive team, standing shoulder-to-shoulder with colleagues.

Together, they would be an unbreakable unit, ready to answer every call, to bravely serve and protect the community she cherished, rescuing those in peril, extinguishing fires, and offering comfort in times of crisis.

As her car glided through the familiar streets back home, each storefront, every tree-lined sidewalk, every passing face seemed to hum with a quiet, almost conspiratorial promise of a future she had not just *dreamed* of, but meticulously *built towards* for so long.

She felt utterly electrified, not just by the prospect of a new career but by the potential of a path that promised to be intensely challenging, undeniably demanding, yet also deeply fulfilling, aligning perfectly with her deepest desire to make a tangible difference in the lives of others. The world outside her bedroom window, once just scenery, now shimmered with infinite possibilities for her future as a firefighter.

11

Anticipation

The ambiance in their deep friendship felt thick with unspoken hope, each shared glance between Aileen and Michael carrying the understood question: *Any news yet?* Both of them were held in that peculiar limbo of post-application waiting, their individual futures, and by extension, their shared one, hanging delicately in the balance.

For Aileen, the stakes were personal. The firefighter spot in Applewood wasn't just a job; it was the culmination of a lifelong dream, a conclusion of her strong sense of purpose and her grueling journey through the fire academy. Applewood, a close-knit community set amidst rolling hills and ocean-side coast, represented the ideal place for her to dedicate her strength and courage and join her proud father on the force. She envisioned herself, helmet in hand, part of a team, making a tangible difference. The thought of receiving that call, the one offering her one of the open positions, sent a potent mix of exhilaration and terror through her very being.

Michael, meanwhile, was holding his breath for a different kind of future. His applied-for finance position for a national bank in the bustling town of Garrison offered the stability and professional growth he craved. It was a step up, a chance to build a more secure foundation for them both, to contribute meaningfully to their long-term plans. Garrison, relatively close to Applewood, would allow them to build a life together without an impossible commute, a practical consideration that weighed heavily on his mind. He envisioned the quiet satisfaction of a steady career, of contributing to their financial security, even as he secretly admired Aileen's more outwardly heroic aspirations.

The past few weeks had been a blur of early mornings and late nights for Aileen, the fire academy demanding every ounce of her physical and mental energy. The rigorous training, the theoretical exams, the drills that pushed her to her limits – all had left little room for anything else.

Michael had felt her absence keenly; his apartment, usually filled with their easy banter and shared routines, had been eerily quiet, punctuated only by his solitary evenings. Their conversations had been only seized fragments, often over crackling phone lines, punctuated by Aileen's exhaustion or Michael's quiet longing for her return to more familiar normalcy.

Now, with the academy behind them and the waiting game for both of them in full swing, they were deliberately, perhaps even desperately, trying to mend the frayed edges of their relationship. They cooked dinners together at his place, the clinking of pots and pans a comforting rhythm.

They took long, aimless walks through the local park, hands intertwined, savoring the simple act of physical closeness they had missed. Some evenings, he would spend time at her home, just watching TV together.

They talked, not just about their job prospects, but about everything and nothing – rekindling the intimacy and everyday companionship that had been sacrificed on the altar of Aileen's ambition. And yet, even as they laughed and shared stories, a subtle current of anxiety lay hidden beneath the surface, a reminder that their newly reclaimed togetherness was still contingent on the news that could drop at any moment, shaping their future in ways they could have only imagined.

After a particularly delightful dinner with her family at home one evening, Michael, completely out of the blue, pulled his vintage, dark blue sedan into the driveway of the Byrne residence. The air was remarkably crisp for the season that evening, hinting at the subtle shift towards the coming winter, and overhead, the vast canvas of the sky was utterly ablaze with a multitude of stars, each one a diamond pinprick in the infinite velvet expanse. He asked Aileen to step outside and get into his car for a talk.

With a shared glance that spoke volumes, Aileen settled into the comfortable front seat beside him, the scent of her subtle perfume a delicate counterpoint to the clean, cool night air. "Where are we going, Michael?" she asked curiously. He answered, with a mysterious grin, "You'll see."

He then navigated the winding coastal roads with practiced ease as they eventually descended towards their cherished lookout point: the rugged promontory overlooking the entrance to the Applewood harbor. This was their safe space, a place where the world seemed to fall away, leaving only the vastness of nature and the quiet intimacy of their connection.

As he turned off the engine, plunging them into a sudden silence, they both fell instantly captivated by the rhythmic, undulating sweep of the Atlantic Ocean. Its mighty breath was a constant, soothing murmur against the rocky shore, a deep, ancient sound that swallowed all other anxieties.

Above them, the heavens glittered with an almost impossible brilliance; the Milky Way, a shimmering river of stardust, was faintly discernible, creating an awe-inspiring celestial dome. Below, painting a luminous path across the dark, mercurial waters, the navigational buoys flashed their sentinel-like red and green beacons, a steady, hypnotic pulse against the inky blackness, guiding unseen vessels toward safety.

The entire panorama was truly enchanting, a scene straight out of a dream. And to crown this already magnificent spectacle, a large, burnished full moon was just beginning its majestic ascent over the eastern horizon. It cast a warm, golden-orange glow that slowly bled into a soft, ethereal silver as it climbed, painting a shimmering pathway across the water and bathing the entire scene in a mystical, otherworldly radiance.

Nestled closely within the warm confines of the car's front bench seat, Aileen's head resting comfortably on Michael's shoulder, his arm a secure anchor around her, the two soulmates savored the romantic scenery before them. It was a moment of perfect stillness, broken only by the ocean's gentle growl and the soft rumble of their own heartbeats.

With an unbiased candor forged through years of shared trust and mutual respect, they began a conversation that drifted effortlessly between the past and the present. They spoke, with raw and sometimes deep emotions, of their individual struggles – the lonely battles fought, the doubts weathered, the moments of despair that had once threatened to engulf them.

They recounted the triumphs, too, the quiet victories that had shaped them into the resilient, compassionate individuals they now were. Their present situation, in stark contrast, felt like a peaceful harbor after a storm.

The discussion then naturally, almost inevitably, turned to the future. They talked, at some length, about their shared aspirations, the dreams they intertwined and nurtured together, and the practicalities of building a life together. The conversation, though serious, was infused with a giddy excitement as they dared to articulate their thoughts for eventual nuptials.

While they still considered themselves young adults, with careers still building and lives still being shaped, in their hearts and minds, their path forward seemed not just desirable but truly inevitable. Their connection was a force of nature, too strong, too genuine, to be denied or diverted.

It was during this heavenly night, with the ocean's timeless song as their backdrop, that Aileen, with a hint of vulnerability coloring her tone, somewhat hesitantly broached a topic she had kept fiercely guarded from Michael for so long. She spoke of the mysterious, secret whisper that had, from time to time, for the past few years, subtly, almost imperceptibly, guided her. It wasn't a true auditory voice, she explained, but an undeniable, intuitive, barely-there hushed tone, a quiet certainty in moments of confusion or significant decision-making, a sense of rightness that had never led her astray.

Michael listened intently, his gaze unwavering, free of judgment or alarm. When she finished, a soft smile played on his lips. "You know, it's good to have something, or someone, that you believe is guiding you," he responded, his voice a soothing balm against her lingering apprehension. He paused, his gaze sweeping across the vast, star-strewn ocean, then settled back on her. "Everyone yearns to have direction, Aileen. We all seek meaning, a compass for our lives, whether it's faith, philosophy, family, or even just an inner sense of knowing. This is just yours."

His acceptance was absolute, a validation that reassured her to her very soul, strengthening the already unbreakable bond between them as they turned their eyes back to the shimmering, moonlit sea, ready for whatever direction their inevitable future might unveil.

The clock slowly edged past midnight, signaling the inevitable conclusion to their intense discussion, so Michael and Aileen finally decided it was time to head back. After a quiet drive through the deserted, lamp-lit streets, Michael dropped Aileen off at her house, exchanging a brief, knowing smile and kiss that acknowledged the depth of their exchange before she disappeared inside. Cruising the final few blocks to his own apartment, the initial fatigue quickly gave way to a sense of satisfaction; he felt intensely glad they had finally peeled back the layers of their complex distress, leaving him feeling lighter and more understanding as he finally pulled into his parking spot.

A week or so later, the phone rang, and Aileen was delighted to hear Michael's voice on the other end, brimming with an energy she immediately recognized as good news. He wasted no time sharing his excitement: he'd been accepted for the bank position in Garrison! The relief and joy in his voice were unmistakable as he detailed his start date—the early on the following Monday morning—emphasizing the "8:00 A.M. sharp" as if he already had his suit picked out. His excitement practically buzzed through the phone line, a clear indication that this new chapter was exactly what he'd been hoping for. Aileen replied, "That's awesome, Michael. Glad you got what you wanted." Then added, "We should celebrate! But wait... Guess what?"

Bubbling with excitement after hearing Michael's wonderful news about his new position, Aileen was practically bursting to share her own triumph: she, too, had just received a fantastic phone call, having been confirmed for one of the coveted open positions on the Applewood Fire Department roster! Her new role would commence in a remarkably short time frame, necessitating immediate action on her part.

She would first need to travel to a tailor in Garrison to be meticulously fitted for a complete set of official firefighter uniforms, including both her service attire and dress blues.

Following this, she was scheduled to report to the central fire station to be sized for all her tactical gear – specifically, her firefighter steel-toed boots, specialized pants, turnout coat, gloves, Nomex hood, and of course, her helmet. It was at this station visit that she would also be officially assigned her unique department number, marking her full integration into the department's team.

The following day, the gentle, slow rise of Saturday morning bathed the Byrne household in a golden, inviting light. The kitchen hummed with the usual weekend symphony of clattering cutlery, sizzling bacon, and the cheerful, sometimes boisterous, chatter of a family waking up. As everyone eventually gravitated to their seats around the old oak kitchen table, in the course of the casual morning pandemonium – Sean attempting to balance a sugar cube on his nose, Aileen recounting a faded dream, and Faith expertly navigating the coffee maker – Liam cleared his throat. His voice, calm and warm, cut through the joyous chaos.

"Alright, everyone, settle down for a moment," he announced, a genial smile playing on his lips. "What does everyone think about us dining out tonight to celebrate all the great news we've all received lately?" He paused, letting the suggestion hang in the air, then brightened. "We can go to that nice lobster house in town, you know, the Harbor's Edge, and really have a feast. On us!" A ripple of excited whispers and happy exclamations went through the table, and a chorus of enthusiastic agreement followed. Hands, big and small, shot up into the air, seals of unanimous approval. Then, Aileen, ever thoughtful of her boyfriend, piped up, "Dad, can Michael come along too?" A warm smile touched his lips. "Sure! He's practically part of the family at this point, so of course he can join us."

As dusk settled into twilight and the stars began to pepper the darkening sky, the entire Byrne party, now grown even larger, made their way to the elegant Harbor's Edge restaurant. The establishment buzzed with a sophisticated yet convivial energy, the soft clinking of glassware mingling with hushed conversations. They were led to a grand, circular table set in a semi-private alcove in a corner of the dining room, providing both intimacy and a view of the bustling room. It was a perfect setting to commemorate the joyous occasion.

The whole Byrne family was there in full force: Aileen's father, Liam, radiating quiet, proud satisfaction; her elegant mother, Faith, with a sparkle in her eyes; her mischievous younger brother, Sean, already eyeing the breadbasket with predatory focus. Beside them sat Michael, Aileen's steadfast sweetheart, looking a bit shy but undeniably pleased to be included, accompanied by his friendly mother, Judy Brown. And to complete the festive circle, Aileen's beloved older aunts and uncles from both sides of the family had also joined, creating a vibrant energy of kinship and affection.

The air soon filled with the rich aroma of melted butter and fresh seafood as platters laden with glistening lobster tails, steamed mussels, and perfectly seared scallops arrived, promising a truly memorable meal.

Glasses, filled with sparkling cider for the younger ones and a crisp white wine for the adults, clinked together as celebratory toasts were given. Liam raised his glass first, his voice resonating with gratitude, speaking of family, health, the promising future ahead, and the awesome new addition to the Applewood fire department. Others followed, their words weaving a tapestry of shared memories and hopes.

Laughter, easy conversation, and the comfortable rhythm of a family truly connected filled the space. Stories were swapped, jokes were told, and even Sean managed to impress with a particularly witty remark, earning a rare nod of approval from Liam. As the last remnants of dessert were cleared and the rich scent of coffee mingled with the salty air, a profound sense of peace settled over them all. The world, indeed, felt perfectly aligned, brimming with love, good fortune, and the undeniable warmth of family.

12

The Proposal

The cold air of early winter carried both the faint scent of fallen leaves and the sharp tang of apprehension as Aileen and Michael embarked on their new professional journeys.

For Aileen, the uniform of the Applewood Fire Department felt both a heavy responsibility and a badge of honor. Her first assignment, as a newly minted private, placed her at the quiet, unassuming one-truck substation on the outskirts of town on Main Street, just down the road from her home. It was the same substation that she and Maya passed by on their way back from their excursion into the forest a while back.

Each fire station operates on an unwavering principle of perpetual readiness, maintaining continuous coverage every single hour of every day. This critical 24/7 vigilance is upheld by a dedicated crew of three highly trained firefighters who are physically present and on shift at all times. This essential trio typically comprises an officer, or replacement acting officer (who leads the crew and handles incident command), a driver/operator (responsible for operating the fire apparatus and its complex systems), and a firefighter. These two firefighters swap duties each shift.

This round-the-clock manning is expertly managed through a meticulously structured rotation involving three distinct shifts – A, B, and C. Rather than working standard 8-hour or 12-hour days, these crews serve demanding 24-hour shifts. For example, Shift A might be on duty from 8 AM on Monday until 8 AM on Tuesday. On Tuesday morning, Shift B seamlessly takes over for its 24-hour tour, followed by Shift C on Wednesday. Then, on Thursday morning, the cycle precisely repeats with Shift A returning to duty.

Consequently, this system ensures that each specific shift crew (A, B, or C) is on active duty every third day. Crucially, after completing their intensive 24-hour rotation, each crew benefits from two full, consecutive days (approximately 48 hours) off-duty. This extended break affords them essential time for deep rest and recovery from the significant physical and mental demands of their job, personal appointments, family life, and crucial ongoing training.

Firefighters also had a unique arrangement when it came to their downtime. While they were given 48-hour breaks between shifts, it didn't necessarily mean they were completely off the hook. In reality, they were still considered "on call" during this time off, which meant they could be summoned back to duty at a moment's notice if a significant incident occurred that required additional personnel.

This meant that even when they were technically off duty, they still had to be prepared to jump into action, whether that meant rushing to a fire, responding to a rescue call, or providing backup to their colleagues. As a result, their breaks were often filled with a sense of anticipation, knowing that their rest could be disrupted at any time, and they had to be ready to spring into action to serve their community.

Despite the unpredictability of their schedules, these brave men and women took it all in stride, always putting the needs of others before their own, and demonstrating a level of dedication that was truly inspiring.

This sub-station, however, hums with a low-level readiness, a stark contrast to the bustling main central station, but one where every piece of equipment and the big red fire truck was meticulously maintained. Aileen's days were filled with the routines of a firefighter's life – answering emergency calls, checking hoses, maintaining the apparatus, honing her skills in simulated scenarios, and the ever-present, almost meditative, cleaning of the station. The fire officer and his team would take turns preparing diverse meals in the modest kitchen. Each firefighter had his or her own bunk room where they could rest and have some valuable privacy.

Meanwhile, a few miles away in the more established town of Garrison, Michael took up his post as the newly hired financial officer at the local bank. The polished mahogany of his desk gleamed under the fluorescent lights, a testament to the seriousness and gravity of his new domain. His world was one of spreadsheets, financial reports, and the intricate dance of numbers. The weight of his new responsibilities settled upon him quickly, a burden of trust and precision.

As the initial excitement of their new beginnings began to fade, the relentless march of weeks bled into months. Both Aileen and Michael found their respective roles to be far more demanding than they had initially expected. The relentless pace, the constant need for vigilance, and the sheer mental fortitude required for their jobs began to take a toll.

For Aileen, the adrenaline of responding to calls competed with the long stretches of quiet, punctuated by the ever-present awareness of potential danger.

For Michael, the intricate calculations and the constant scrutiny of his work created a persistent tone of anxiety in the background. Yet, with each passing day, amidst the stress and the strain, a quiet strength began to emerge within them both. They were learning to navigate the pressures, their determination hardening like tempered steel.

Aileen, surprisingly, found herself looking forward to the jarring, insistent blare of the fire alarms. These sudden disruptions, while signaling potential danger and demanding immediate, decisive action, offered a welcome respite from the routine. They were opportunities, not to be feared, but to be embraced. Each alarm was a chance to shed the rookie tag and to prove her worth to her seasoned colleagues. It was a chance to translate the theoretical knowledge painstakingly absorbed at the Academy into tangible, life-saving skills.

The controlled chaos of a fire scene, the rush of adrenaline, the coordinated teamwork – these were the moments where she felt most alive, most useful, and where she could truly execute the applied fire-ground operations that had become second nature.

Michael, however, experienced a different kind of internal battle. While he had successfully navigated the initial wave of apprehension, the insidious need for absolute perfection continued to dog him. The digital readouts on his computer screen were his constant companions, each digit a potential pitfall. The knowledge that even a minuscule miscalculation could have significant, detrimental consequences for the bank, its clients, and his own burgeoning career cast a long shadow over his work. The pressure wasn't just about doing a good job; it was about achieving an unassailable level of accuracy, a standard of flawless execution that felt increasingly elusive, yet absolutely imperative.

Therefore, with the months imperceptibly bleeding into years, a comfortable rhythm began to settle over their lives. Michael and Aileen, each now firmly established in their separate professional spheres and individual routines, had forged a relationship that, while deeply connected, still maintained its distinct boundaries. He was flourishing in his career, she in hers, and their shared moments were precious, albeit confined to their individual living spaces.

A quiet conviction had, however, begun to coalesce within Michael. This burgeoning certainty, a sense that their journey demanded a grander, more permanent chapter, remained a closely guarded secret from Aileen.

He'd watched her, listened to her, felt the undeniable pull of their connection deepen with every passing moment, and he knew, with a certainty that both thrilled and terrified him, that the couple was clearly ready for the next monumental move in their relationship. Marriage, with its promises of shared futures and lifelong partnership, now occupied the forefront of his conscience mind.

The decision finally made, the execution became the terrifying hurdle. Weeks, perhaps even months, were spent in an internal battle of courage and apprehension, waiting for the precise time. He rehearsed the words in his head, imagined every possible reaction, and wrestled with his nerves. Finally, after one particularly anxious late afternoon when Aileen was out to dinner with some of her friends in Garrison, he built up enough uneasy, almost frantic courage to approach Liam Byrne, Aileen's father.

From his small, cluttered apartment, bathed in the dim glow of a streetlamp filtering through the dusty blinds, Michael's hand trembled as he dialed the familiar number for the Byrne residence. Each ring echoed with a nervous urgency in the quiet room. He took a deep, shaky breath as the phone was finally answered on the other end, a warm, maternal voice cutting through his anxiety. "Hello?"

"Faith? It's Michael," he managed, his voice a little hoarser than he intended.

"Oh, Michael, hello dear," Faith replied, her tone friendly but with a hint of curiosity. "How are you?"

"I'm... I'm alright, Mrs. Byrne, thank you. Is Aileen there?" Michael asked, a flicker of hope igniting, quickly extinguished by her response.

Faith chuckled lightly. "No, dear, Aileen's out. She's gone for an evening meal with some of her friends. Just getting some downtime, you know."

A knot tightened in Michael's stomach, but he pressed on, his gaze fixed on the swirling patterns of dust motes dancing in the faint light. "Ah, I see. Well, actually, Mrs. Byrne, the reason I'm calling is... I was hoping I could come over and have a word with your husband, Liam, if that's at all possible?" He paused, gathering his courage. "It's, uh, it's a rather serious matter, and I really feel it would be best to discuss it in person, face-to-face, if that's alright with you." The words tumbled out, a little rushed, a little desperate.

Faith's tone shifted, becoming more accommodating. "Liam? Oh, yes, that could certainly work. He's actually free this evening, you know. He doesn't have to be in at the fire station tomorrow, so he's got a bit of a stay-in planned. He'll probably just be puttering around at home, maybe watch the late show on TV later on." She paused, considering. "Yes, that would be fine. You could come over after 6:30 pm. Why don't you aim for around then? I'll let him know you're coming, and I'll watch out for you when you arrive."

A wave of relief washed over Michael, so potent it made his knees feel weak. "Thank you, Faith, I mean Mrs. Byrne. Thank you so much. I really appreciate it." He hung up the phone, the click of the receiver sounding unnaturally loud. The weight of what he had to say to Liam hadn't lessened, but now, at least, he had an opportunity to say it.

It was a semi-formal affair, a moment steeped in tradition and expectation. After Faith Byrne welcomed him into their home, Michael found Liam in the living room, the scent of old books and the aroma of warm cocoa hanging faintly in the air, a setting that only heightened the solemnity of the occasion. Michael entered and sat down on the sofa nearby, facing Liam.

His palms were damp, and he placed his hands on his knees, leaning forward, his heart thumping a frantic rhythm against his ribs as he began to speak, carefully articulating his intentions. He brought up his "unwavering confidence in their deep love for one another," emphasizing not just a fleeting passion, but a mature, enduring affection that had weathered time and the minor storms.

He explained, with a sincerity that hopefully trumped his visible nervousness, that he believed they "were ready for the next logical step" - a natural, inevitable progression for a bond as profound as theirs.

Michael swiftly moved to the practicalities, showcasing his foresight and sense of responsibility. He assured Liam that his current apartment, while a bachelor pad for years, offered more than enough room for the two of them, for now, to comfortably start their married life together.

He'd already mentally rearranged furniture, envisioned shared breakfasts in the sun-drenched kitchen, and imagined their combined possessions finding a home within its walls. Furthermore, with their combined wages – Aileen's promising income added to his own stable earnings – he was entirely sure they had a solid, robust financial foundation for a long-term commitment, not just of love, but of secure living.

It was an argument built on both heart and prudence, a plea for a father's blessing rooted in affection and careful planning.

After considerable, deep deliberation, Liam finally summoned his wife, Faith, into the living room, where she joined Michael and himself to discuss the delicate matter at hand. The trio engaged in a lengthy and earnest conversation regarding the impending proposal, with Liam and Faith carefully assessing Michael's intentions and plans.

Ultimately, the Byrnes, satisfied by the sincerity and thoughtful presentation Michael had made, gave their heartfelt approval, agreeing that he could, indeed, formally propose to their beloved daughter, Aileen.

Standing tall, Michael extended a hand to each of them, his posture conveying both gratitude and a respectful acknowledgment of the responsibility they now entrusted to him. His voice steady, he looked them in the eye and promised, with every fiber of his being, to love, cherish, and forever protect their precious daughter.

With their blessing and their hearts visibly reassured by his sincerity, Michael exited the quiet warmth of their home and made his way to his car. The moment his car door clicked shut and he was safely inside, the carefully contained emotion erupted in a mighty, boisterous, "Yes! Thank you!" that echoed briefly in the night, a triumphant exclamation of joy and relief.

At that precise moment, miles away in Garrison, the bustling cafe clamor faded into a distant hum as Aileen, deeply immersed in a spirited discussion with her friends Maya and Georgia, suddenly felt it – a familiar, ethereal whisper brushing against her ear. Again, it wasn't a sound anyone else could perceive, but to her, the words were crystal clear, resonating with an almost tangible warmth: *'Something exciting and wonderful is on the way!'*

A subtle shiver traced its way down her spine, and she involuntarily shook her head, a brief flicker of suspicious wonder crossing her face as she pondered the cryptic message. Despite the sudden, otherworldly interruption, Aileen quickly composed herself, her attention smoothly snapping back to the lively exchange at the table, a tiny, secret smile playing on her lips as she rejoined the discussion, the whisper's promise a soft hum beneath her consciousness.

That very weekend, driven by the intention to propose, Michael journeyed to Garrison, determined to find an affordable yet stylish diamond engagement ring. He envisioned proposing to Aileen during a romantic candlelight dinner at his apartment, and upon entering the jewelry store, he headed directly to the diamond ring display.

A dazzling array of styles greeted him, from traditional round and elegant emerald to unique pear and marquise cuts, each promising distinct aesthetics and sparkle. After a thorough discussion with the knowledgeable saleslady about the various styles and price points, he ultimately chose a classic gold band in Aileen's size, adorned with a heart-shaped diamond, believing that it would perfectly symbolize the profound, heartfelt love he shared with her.

The hum of the engine was a nervous counterpoint to Michael's racing heart as he drove back home from Garrison, the weight of the small, black velvet box in his jacket pocket a tangible symbol of the immense responsibility he was about to embrace with Aileen. The closer he got to his familiar tenement building, the more the stark question, "What if she says no?" echoed in his mind, a chilling tremor running down his spine.

But as he stepped into the quiet of his apartment, the fear began to subside, replaced by a warm flood of memories – the laughter on spontaneous road trips, the shared vulnerability of late-night conversations, the electrifying intimacy that had blossomed between them.

He recalled the spark that ignited the moment when they met on that trail in the woods so many years ago, the adventures they had already shared, and the deep well of affection that had grown into an unshakable certainty.

They were meant to be. With renewed confidence, Michael spent the evening tidying and arranging his living space, preparing not just his home, but his heart, for the new chapter he was so eager to begin with Aileen.

The morning dawned with an almost ethereal brilliance, a crystal-clear canvas painted with the softest of golds and pinks as the sun climbed above the horizon. For Aileen, this particular day was a rare and welcome gift – a day off from the exhilarating, yet demanding, rhythm of her shifts at the fire station. She savored the quiet stillness at home, and the aroma of freshly brewed coffee still lingering in the air, when her phone buzzed, a bright chime cutting through the tranquility. It was Michael. His voice, warm and laced with an easy charm, carried a hint of playful suggestion.

He suggested a dinner for two that evening at his place, an invitation that immediately sparked a flicker of pleasant curiosity within her. He described it simply as a "nice dinner," but Aileen, who knew Michael well, sensed a subtle undertone, a promise of something more intimate, more special. She agreed with the 'date' and said that she'd be there.

As the afternoon sun began its descent, casting long shadows and painting the sky in hues of orange and purple, she had dressed up somewhat for the occasion and even put her hair in a bun instead of her usual ponytails. Aileen then navigated her way to Michael's apartment building.

The clock on her dashboard read precisely 6:00 PM when she pulled into the complex. The parking lot, usually a bustling hub of activity, was surprisingly quiet that evening, and she easily found an open space bathed in the soft glow of a streetlamp.

Stepping out of the car, she took a deep breath, the crisp evening air invigorating her senses. The building itself was a familiar structure, and she readily made her way to the entrance. The ascent up the stairwell to Michael's second-floor apartment was punctuated by the rhythmic echo of her footsteps, each step carrying her closer to an unknown anticipation. There was a certain ambiguity to her excitement, a delightful uncertainty that buzzed beneath her skin.

With a soft, yet deliberate, rap of her knuckles against the door, Aileen announced her arrival. The silence that followed was brief, barely a breath, before the door swung open with surprising speed. Michael stood there, his face illuminated by a wide, infectious grin that crinkled the corners of his eyes. He was impeccably dressed, a crisp sports coat draped over a neatly pressed shirt, his tie knotted with a subtle elegance. "Aileen," he exclaimed, his voice resonating with genuine warmth as he pulled the door wider. "You're here!"

The greeting was met with a spontaneous embrace, their bodies fitting together as if they were made for each other. A quick, affectionate kiss sealed the reunion, a silent acknowledgment of their shared affection. He gently took her coat, his fingers brushing hers as he hung it with care on a dark, polished wood coat rack by the entrance.

As Michael guided her into the apartment, Aileen's gaze was immediately drawn to the kitchen area. It was a cozy, inviting space, bathed in a soft, flickering luminescence. Dozens of small, elegant candles were strategically placed throughout the room, their gentle flames dancing and casting mesmerizing shadows on the walls.

The air was subtly perfumed with their faint, waxy scent, mingling with an enticing aroma of something delicious cooking. "What's up, Michael?" she asked, her voice tinged with a playful curiosity, the candlelit ambiance adding an air of mystery to her question. He responded not with words, but with a slow, knowing smile, his eyes twinkling as he extended a hand, gesturing towards the dining table.

She followed his unspoken invitation, settling into a comfortable chair at the small, candlelit table. The setting was undeniably romantic, a deliberate and thoughtful creation. As she adjusted her position, Michael's gaze met hers, his expression earnest and full of emotion.

In a move that caught her completely off guard, he slowly lowered himself down onto one knee beside her. A hushed gasp escaped her lips as his hand reached out, gently taking hers. From the breast pocket of his sports coat, he produced a small, black velvet box. With a practiced, steady motion, he opened it, revealing a dazzling engagement ring, its heart-shaped diamond catching the candlelight and scattering tiny rainbows across the table.

Aileen's mind reeled, caught in a whirlwind of shock and utter bewilderment. The unexpectedness of the moment stole her breath. In that instant, her thoughts flashed back to a seemingly insignificant encounter just a few nights prior, in that quaint cafe in Garrison. A hushed whisper, a fleeting voice she couldn't quite place, had murmured, '*Something wonderful is on the way!*'

At the time, she had dismissed it as a fanciful thought, a stray observation. But now, gazing at Michael, at the ring, at the sheer love radiating from his eyes, she knew. This was it. This was the wonderful thing.

Michael's voice, when he finally spoke, was a deep, resonant rumble, filled with an overwhelming sincerity. "Aileen," he began, his grip on her hand tightening slightly, "I love you with all my heart and soul, and I want to spend the rest of my life with you. Will you please do me the wonderful honor and be my wife?" The question hung in the air, suspended in the flickering candlelight.

Aileen took a deep, steadying breath, allowing the immensity of the moment to wash over her. The surprise had subsided, replaced by a surge of pure, unadulterated joy. Tears welled in her eyes, not of sadness, but of overwhelming happiness and love. She leaned forward, her heart overflowing, and wrapped her arms around his neck, pulling him into an emotional embrace. Their lips met in a kiss that spoke volumes, a promise of a lifetime of shared moments. "Yes!" she whispered against his lips, her voice thick with emotion. "Oh, Michael, yes! I love you, too. Of course, I'll marry you!" The thought of becoming "Mrs. Aileen Brown" bloomed in her mind, and she smiled at the sound of it, a perfect, harmonious match.

With trembling fingers, Michael slid the ring onto her finger. It settled there with a perfect, satisfying pop, a symbol of their eternal commitment. It fit as if it had been custom-made, a flawless culmination of love, anticipation, and a wonderfully realized dream.

The air in Michael's apartment, still humming with the joyous energy of the proposal, took on a warm, comforting glow as he transitioned from heartfelt declarations to domestic delights. The clinking of cutlery against ceramic plates marked the beginning of a new chapter, one seasoned with the rich aroma of his meticulously prepared spaghetti and meatball dinner. The pasta itself was perfectly tender, but firm, coated in a savory, slow-simmered marinara sauce that had been a labor of love, and the handcrafted meatballs had the aroma of ancient Italy. Alongside the main dinner, a crisp, vibrant salad offered a refreshing counterpoint, its medley of fresh greens, cherry tomatoes, and a light vinaigrette a proof of Michael's attention to detail. And as the centerpiece of the meal, a deep, ruby-red bottle of Merlot stood ready, its complex bouquet promising to enhance every bite with its smooth, velvety flavor.

As they savored the meal, the conversation flowed as effortlessly as the wine. Hours melted away as they rediscovered each other in this new, committed light, their laughter and shared glances weaving a tapestry of affection.

The initial excitement of the engagement gradually deepened into a shared vision of their future together. They spoke of wedding plans, of the ceremony, the reception, and the myriad of details that would soon fill their days with happiness.

Michael, ever the planner, had already laid the groundwork for their life after the vows. He revealed that with the lease secured for the entire year, Aileen could seamlessly move into his apartment once they were married.

This practical consideration opened up a world of possibilities, transforming the spare bedroom from a mere afterthought into a versatile space. It could become Michael's dedicated study, allowing him to focus on his financial work, or a creative office for Aileen to pursue her passions, or perhaps a well-equipped weight room for them to maintain their health and well-being together. The prospect of this shared space, a tangible symbol of their union, added another layer of excitement to their burgeoning plans.

Once the last trace of the delicious meal had been cleared, and with their hearts full and their minds buzzing with dreams, Aileen felt an irresistible urge to share her momentous news. Her family, blissfully unaware of the life-altering event that had just transpired, awaited her return.

With a final, lingering look at Michael, a silent promise of their future hanging in the air between them, she eagerly headed back home, ready to unleash the joyous surprise that would undoubtedly ripple through her family's household.

13

The Wedding

At home, the old grandfather clock in the hall chimed eleven-thirty, its resonant declaration echoing through the hushed house, as Aileen burst through the side door. Her cheeks were flushed, her eyes alight with an incandescent joy that instantly banished any trace of the late hour. Barely shedding her coat, she raced with an almost giddy abandon into the warm, inviting glow of the kitchen.

There, bathed in the soft, yellow light of a single lamp, her father, Liam, sat at the sturdy oak kitchen table, savoring the last comforting sips of a late-night mug of cocoa, the comforting aroma of chocolate and steam still clinging to the air. The rest of the household was already deep in slumber; her younger brother, Sean, and their mother, Faith, had long since retired to the quiet sanctuary of their second-floor bedrooms, leaving the house in a peaceful, drowsy state.

Aileen, unable to contain the overwhelming news, practically vibrated with excitement. Her smile, brilliant and wide, stretched from ear to ear, a beacon of pure elation. "Dad!" she practically squealed, her voice barely containing the triumphant tremor. "Michael proposed to me tonight, and I said yes!" The words tumbled out in a single, breathless rush.

Liam, momentarily startled by her sudden entrance and the joyous eruption, slowly set his mug down. A flicker of surprise crossed his face, quickly melting into an even wider, deeply knowing grin. He rose from his chair, his movements swift and sure, pulling Aileen into a bear hug so tight it nearly lifted her off her feet. "I knew it was coming, sweetheart," he rumbled, a sense of relief and happiness in his voice. "Michael, your mother and I had a long talk about it just a few days ago. We're so thrilled for you both."

Without another word, Liam released her, his eyes still sparkling with paternal pride. He strode purposefully down the short hallway leading to the staircase, his booming voice, usually reserved for boisterous family dinners, suddenly echoing through the quiet house. "Hey, you guys!" he yelled, pitching his voice high enough to penetrate the upstairs rooms. "Come down here! Right now!"

There was a short, bewildered pause from above, a moment of sleep-addled confusion. Then, a startled rustle of bedding, a confused murmur, and a shared gasp of anticipation quickly preceded the unmistakable sound of movement above. First, the heavy thuds of Sean's athletic stride, followed by the lighter, quickening patter of Faith's steps, as they both pounded down the wooden stairway, their curiosity piqued. They tumbled into the hall, eyes wide with a mixture of sleep-fogged confusion and burgeoning excitement, finding Liam still standing there, a triumphant glint in his eye.

He simply pointed towards the kitchen. Without hesitation, they all rushed in, their gazes immediately drawn to Aileen, who stood beaming, her left hand outstretched, proudly displaying the dazzling heart-shaped engagement ring sparkling on her finger under the kitchen light.

Faith, her initial confusion instantly replaced by a wave of happiness, gasped softly, a hand flying to her mouth. Tears welled in her eyes as she enveloped her daughter in a warm, motherly embrace, a tender caress that spoke volumes of love and pride.

After a long, comforting hug, she gently pulled back, taking Aileen's hand to examine the ring with a reverent gaze. "Oh, darling, it's absolutely exquisite," she whispered, her voice thick with emotion. Smiling, her eyes still misty, she hugged Aileen again, a deeper, more intimate embrace this time. "And Michael," she continued, her voice filled with genuine affection, "he's truly a wonderful young man. I couldn't have picked a better partner for you. May your life together be filled with boundless joy and love."

Even Sean, usually the epitome of teenage nonchalance, had a wide, genuinely happy grin on his face, momentarily forgetting his interrupted sleep in the face of his sister's radiant joy. The kitchen, usually a place for quiet late-night snacks, was now vibrant with the shimmering promise of a beautiful new beginning.

Aileen and Michael, their hearts brimming with the excitement of a shared future, soon started on the delightful, albeit demanding, task of arranging their planned springtime wedding. They envisioned a celebration filled with laughter, love, and the cherished presence of their dearest family and friends, a day that perfectly encapsulated their vibrant connection.

After much deliberation and consulting calendars, they eagerly settled on a beautiful Saturday in early June, a date they hoped would bring with it the mild, blooming embrace of the season.

The weeks that followed became a joyful whirlwind of activity, with planning and finalizing reservations consuming their every free waking moment, broken only by Aileen and Michael's work days.

Late-night phone calls coordinating vendors, endless spreadsheets tracking details, and exhilarating venue tours filled their off days and weekends, transforming what could have been stressful into a shared project of love and anticipation. From floral arrangements to tasting menus, every decision was a collaborative step towards their perfect day.

A significant weight was lifted from their shoulders when Aileen's incredibly generous father, Liam, stepped forward one day with a heartfelt offer, agreeing to fully cover the costs of both the wedding ceremony and the subsequent reception. They would only have to pony up for their honeymoon trip. This loving gesture not only provided immense financial relief but also allowed Aileen and Michael to focus on crafting their dream day without compromise. They chose the venerable St. Joseph's church for their ceremony, drawn to its reverence and stunning stained-glass windows that would cast a rainbow of light on their vows, and for the reception, an exquisite local Applewood caterer, renowned for its sophisticated farm-to-table cuisine and the charming, elegant ambiance of its ballroom.

The seemingly simple task of preparing and dispatching wedding invitations was, in reality, a meticulously orchestrated project, carrying both immense practical importance and emotional weight. It began with careful deliberation over the design, aiming for a visual representation that captured the essence of the couple's style and the overall theme of their impending nuptials – whether classic and elegant, modern and minimalist, or rustic and whimsical.

This involved countless hours poring over paper samples, font choices, color palettes, and potential motifs, often collaborating with a stationery designer to bring their vision to life through proofs and revisions.

Once the aesthetic was perfected, the precise wording had to be crafted. This wasn't merely a matter of stating names and dates; it involved navigating traditional etiquette versus personal preference, deciding whether to include parents as hosts, detailing the ceremony and reception times and locations, and clearly outlining RSVP instructions.

Beyond the main invitation, accompanying cards were required: a response card with a self-addressed, stamped envelope for guests to easily reply, and a details card providing practical information about accommodation, transportation, and gift registry.

Finally, the crucial logistics of sending them out involved meticulously addressing each envelope, with carefully printed labels to ensure accuracy and a formal presentation. Correct postage had to be determined for the often-heavier-than-average envelopes, and then, with a mix of relief and growing excitement, the entire batch was personally delivered to the post office by Michael, officially marking the countdown and setting in motion the joyous anticipation for their guests.

The seemingly simple task of preparing and dispatching wedding invitations was a meticulously orchestrated project, carrying both immense practical importance and emotional weight.

It began with careful deliberation over the design, aiming for a visual representation that captured the essence of the couple's style and the overall theme of their impending nuptials.

Once the aesthetics were perfected, the precise wording had to be crafted. This wasn't merely a matter of listing names and dates; it involved navigating between traditional etiquette and personal preference, deciding whether to include parents as hosts, detailing the ceremony and reception times and locations, and clearly outlining RSVP instructions.

Beyond the main invitation, a pair of accompanying cards was required: a self-addressed response card and a details card providing practical information about available accommodations, transportation, and the gift registry.

Finally, the crucial job of sending out each envelope, with carefully printed labels to ensure accuracy and a formal presentation. Then, with a mix of relief and growing excitement, Michael personally delivered the entire batch to the post office, officially marking the countdown and setting in motion the joyous anticipation for their guests.

Beyond the hectic load of wedding logistics, another, equally significant promise took shimmering form in their minds: the honeymoon. A confirmed five-day escape to the sun-kissed shores of Nassau, Bahamas, was soon secured, painting a vivid picture of an idyllic paradise. The very mention of the destination conjured images of powder-soft, ivory beaches stretching endlessly, kissed by the gentle, rhythmic ebb and flow of exceptionally turquoise waters. This vision of sun-drenched tranquility, vibrant coral reefs teeming with life, and evenings filled with romantic dinners under a canopy of stars became a constant, delightful spark of anticipation, a luminous counterpoint to any mounting wedding stress.

Without delay, the crucial step of reserving and fully paying for their flights was completed, a definitive action that transformed a beautiful dream into an absolute certainty, solidifying their impending post-nuptial adventure into an unforgettable chapter of bliss and exploration.

Just as important as the grand escape, the very heart of their support system – their inner circle – was carefully and affectionately solidified. Michael turned to Vince Drake, his best friend from their childhood days, a bond forged over late-night high-school study sessions, countless shared adventures, and mutual respect.

Vince, a man renowned not only for his loyalty but also for his infectious humor and quick wit that could effortlessly lighten any mood and defuse any tension, accepted the crucial role of best man with an enthusiastic grin, clearly honored to stand as Michael's rock on the big day.

For Aileen, there was never any doubt. Her lifelong confidante and closest friend, Maya Fielding, was without question acknowledged as the natural choice for her maid of honor.

Maya, with her impeccably detailed organizational skills that promised to keep everything gracefully on track, and her boundless, infectious warmth that could make anyone feel instantly at ease, was ready to provide not just practical support, but also the much-needed emotional anchor and an endless supply of laughter throughout the entire joyous journey.

So, the fateful day ultimately arrived. From the crisp, sun-drenched noontime light that spilled through the great hall's stained-glass windows, to the soft, anticipatory murmur of arriving guests, the atmosphere was charged with cheer. This wasn't merely a gathering; it was a celebration simmering with love, excitement, and a sense of shared purpose. Laughter mingled with soft chatter, eyes sparkled with affection, and a collective warmth permeated the entire scene.

As the last guest eventually settled, a hushed reverence descended, a respectful silence that spoke volumes of the moment's importance. Then, with a flourish of soft music and the collective intake of breath, the wedding ceremony began.

Dressed in a flowing, beautiful white wedding gown, Aileen began her graceful walk down the aisle, carrying a gorgeous bouquet. Her gaze, serene yet sparkling with emotion, was fixed on one man: Michael, standing tall and undeniably handsome at the altar. He was impeccable in his neatly pressed black tuxedo, the crisp white shirt, and perfectly tied black bow tie, accentuating his strong features. A small, vibrant boutonniere of a single white rose pinned to his lapel was the only splash of color against the dark fabric.

It was a masterpiece of emotional depth and seamless execution. Every movement was graceful, every transition flawless, and the entire flow was imbued with an exquisite, heartfelt sincerity. From the poignant readings delivered by loved ones to the perfectly timed musical interludes, each element felt carefully chosen, acknowledging the couple's unique journey and close connection.

The minister, a figure of calm wisdom and gentle warmth, took to the podium. His voice, a resonant and soothing baritone, filled the space as he began to speak, not just of romantic infatuation, but of the robust, enduring love that forms the bedrock of a marriage.

He painted a beautiful picture of partnership, of two souls deliberately and joyfully choosing to intertwine their destinies, speaking eloquently on the patience, understanding, and support that truly define a lasting bond. He spoke of the privilege it was to witness this sacred union and guided them through the exquisite beauty and significant weight of the vows they were undertaking. He asked them to consider not just the promises made in that moment, but the lifetime of shared mornings, challenges, and triumphs those promises represented.

As the couple turned to face each other, their eyes alight with a mixture of adoration and gentle trepidation, the air thickened with emotion. Each word of their vows, spoken clearly and from the heart, reverberated through the space, a sacred echo of their deepest commitments.

You could feel the collective catch in the guests' throats, the gentle sniffles, as the depth of their devotion washed over everyone present. It was a heartfelt exchange, raw in its honesty and breathtaking in its sincerity, solidifying a bond that was visibly, gloriously real.

The hushed reverence of St. Joseph's church hung heavy in the air, momentarily broken by the soft murmur of excitement. Then, as the minister pronounced them husband and wife, Michael gently pulled Aileen closer, their eyes locking in a promise that transcended words. As their lips met for their first heartfelt, tender kiss as a newlywed couple, a collective sigh rippled through the pews.

The soft click and whir of countless camera shutters, and the glint of an occasional flash, punctuated the moment, capturing their intertwined joy, while discreet sniffles and quiet, happy tears could be heard from proud mothers, beaming relatives, and choked-up friends cheering among the rows. It was a kiss that sealed not just a ceremony, but a lifetime of shared dreams.

As their lips parted, radiant smiles illuminated their faces, a shared triumph gleaming in their eyes. Hand-in-hand, they turned slowly, presenting themselves to their beloved guests. A majestic swell of organ music filled the space as they began their triumphant parade down the aisle, their steps light and joyful. The initial murmurs erupted into a thunderous, boisterous sound of clapping and heartfelt congratulations. Guests rose to their feet, cheering, whistling, and calling out well-wishes, their faces beaming with happiness. Each step was a celebration, a rhythm of new beginnings.

No sooner had they reached the grand, heavy wooden doors of the church than they stepped out into the crisp afternoon air, bathed in natural light. A veritable cascade of rice and colorful confetti rained down upon them, sparkling like jewels as it caught the sunlight. Friends and family, lined up along the steps, launched the celebratory shower with exuberant cheers and laughter, creating a vibrant, swirling cloud around the ecstatic couple. They emerged from the flurry, laughing and shielding their faces playfully, their radiant smiles undimmed by the flurry of tiny grains and paper.

A brief, joyous flurry of posed photographs followed on the picturesque church steps and beneath the graceful archway, the hired photographer expertly directing them amidst the jovial chaos. Then, with a final wave, they were ushered towards a gleaming, impossibly long black limousine, its polished chrome glinting under the sun.

As the doors swung open, revealing plush leather seats and a discreet partition, they sank inside, a shared exhale of relief and giddy excitement. The ride to the reception venue was their first stolen moment of quiet togetherness as a married couple, filled with soft whispers, shared glances, and perhaps another tender, private kiss as the city streets blurred past.

The journey to the reception venue was a transition from solemnity to celebration. Upon arrival, the grand reception hall was a breathtaking spectacle, transformed into an opulent wonderland for the gala occasion.

Twinkling fairy lights draped across the ceiling, casting a warm, magical glow, while elegant candles flickered in mercury glass holders, adding an intimate ambiance. Cascading streamers in the couple's chosen colors adorned doorways and pillars, and vibrant floral arrangements blossomed on every surface.

The undeniable centerpiece, however, was the magnificent, multi-tiered wedding cake, an architectural marvel of delicate frosting and fresh blooms, proudly displayed on the main, crisp linen-covered dining table, drawing admiring gasps from early arrivals. Sparkling crystal, polished silverware, and delicate place settings completed the picture of refined festivity.

Soon, the grand doors of the hall swung open, and the guests, now seated at their exquisitely decorated tables, watched as the newlyweds made their grand entrance to a crescendo of applause.

Once everyone had settled into their places, a magnificent catered meal commenced – a multi-course culinary delight, elegantly served by attentive staff. The clinking of crystal and the murmur of joyful conversation filled the air.

Toasts were made, beginning with heartfelt and humorous speeches from Vince and Maya, followed by eloquent words from the parents. Stories, both tender and comical, were recounted, painting a vivid picture of the couple's journey, eliciting peals of laughter and nostalgic sighs. Everyone present was swept up in the infectious joy of the occasion, savoring delicious food and even better company.

With the last clink of forks against plates, a new wave of celebration began. The traditional cutting of the wedding cake became a playful ceremony, the couple's hands intertwined on the silver knife as cameras flashed once more.

After sharing the first symbolic bite, the music began in earnest. A live band struck up their first melody, calling the newlyweds to the dance floor for their eagerly anticipated first dance, a moment of graceful romance under the twinkling lights.

The air soon vibrated with shared joy and boisterousness. Guest dancing quickly ensued, with attendees of all ages taking to the floor, twirling, jiving, and laughing with abandon. The band transitioned seamlessly between romantic ballads, lively pop hits, and classic dance tunes, ensuring the energy never waned.

More spontaneous toasts were made throughout the afternoon, clinking glasses commemorating friendships, love, and the bright future ahead. The reception hall buzzed with the delightful hum of conversation, the joyful shouts from the dance floor, "Kiss! Kiss!" and the melodic strains of music, creating an unforgettable day of celebration and fellowship.

The last champagne bubbles having been savored, the final heartfelt goodbyes exchanged, and the joyous, whirlwind reception had finally drawn to a close, leaving Michael and Aileen suspended in a delicious exhaustion mingled with pure, unadulterated joy. Hand-in-hand, their fingers intertwined in a clasp that felt both familiar and profoundly new, they carried the lingering buzz of celebration back to Michael's apartment. The quiet hum of the car felt like a decompression chamber after the cacophony of music and laughter, a gentle transition from public spectacle to private intimacy.

Stepping over the threshold, unlocking the door, felt like crossing into a new, beautifully shared chapter. Over the preceding weeks, Aileen had gradually moved some of her cherished belongings – including some needed clothes, her vibrant collection of art, books, a plush throw blanket, some artwork, a whimsical ceramic vase, various trinkets, and a cascade of delicate scarves – weaving them all seamlessly into the fabric of Michael's established space.

Now, the apartment truly breathed with both of their presences, creating a harmonious blend that felt unequivocally theirs.

Her brightly colored kitchen tools settled beside his minimalist gadgets; her overflowing bookshelf now stood shoulder-to-shoulder with his curated vinyl collection.

With a shared, almost ritualistic tenderness, they shed their formal wear. The weighty silk of Aileen's elaborate gown, which had moved with such grace on the dance floor, slipped to the floor in a puddle of cream and lace, replaced by the delightful lightness of soft cotton and worn denim.

Michael, with a sigh of relief, unbuttoned the restrictive collar of his crisp tuxedo, untied his bow tie, and kicked off his polished shoes. In that simple act of undressing, they shed not just fabric, but the last vestiges of public ceremony, embracing the freedom of simply being Aileen and Michael Brown, husband and wife, in the comfort of their own home.

A knowing glance passed between them, a silent acknowledgment of the journey just completed and the adventure lying ahead. With renewed energy, propelled by an undercurrent of excitement that had been building for months, they gathered their pared-down luggage – two sleek, carry-on bags and two rolling suitcases, carefully packed with tropical essentials and the promise of endless sun-drenched days.

The Applewood telephone poles blurred past as they drove through the quiet, late-afternoon streets towards the bustling Portland Airport.

The low, constant thrum of jet engines idling outside provided a deep bass note, overlaid by the staccato rhythm of rolling suitcases and the muffled, echoing announcements from distant gates. As they settled near their boarding zone, the fluorescent lights cast a hazy, yet exciting glow over the polished floors, illuminating the mixture of weary and elated faces waiting for their own escapes.

For the newlyweds, this frantic energy was comforting; every security chatter and hurried step was merely the organized commotion necessary to propel them toward turquoise waters and white sands, already tasting the salty air of the Caribbean just beyond the darkened glass.

The powerful roar of the engines soon became a comforting hum as their plane lifted off from Portland, leaving behind the crisp night air for the promise of southern warmth.

The initial leg of their journey carried them south to Miami, Florida. There, they indulged in a luxurious overnight stay at a grand, retro-inspired hotel, a sumptuous suite offering a taste of the indulgence to come. They sank into plush linens, the soft rustle of palm trees outside their window a gentle lullaby, their dreams already filled with turquoise waters.

The next morning, refreshed and eager, they caught a short, exhilarating flight, the final, thrilling leg of their journey, directly to the sun-kissed shores of Nassau, the turquoise expanse of the Caribbean already visible teasingly from their airborne window.

14

The Attic

Nassau wasn't just everything Aileen and Michael had envisioned; it was a vibrant, living canvas that surpassed their wildest romantic dreams, an opulent and untamed paradise crafted with exquisite precision for the singular purpose of fostering romance and serene relaxation. Time, that relentless master, seemed to surrender its dominion in this idyllic setting. Days blurred into seamless sun-drenched bliss and effortless joy, each hour melting into the next with a languid grace that defied the outside world. Their itinerary wasn't dictated by clocks, but by the ebb and flow of their desires, a constant stream of immersive activities punctuated by moments of delicious idleness.

Evenings unfolded under a velvet sky, studded with a billion pinpoint stars that seemed to twinkle just for them.

They gravitated towards the infectious pulse of live island music—the lilting steel pan, the insistent beat of the drums, the soulful strains of a calypso guitar. Barefoot on the soft, warm sand of a beach-side bar, their bodies swayed in unison, a silent conversation unfolding between them as the music seeped into their very souls.

The balmy, salt-kissed breeze wasn't just warm; it was a gentle caress carrying the faint scent of tropical blossoms and the ocean, blessing their union with its soft presence.

Culinary journeys awaited them each night. Fine dining establishments, often open-air and kissed by the gentle sea air, presented menus that celebrated the island's bounty. Flickering candlelight cast a golden glow over intimate tables, illuminating plates laden with the freshest, most succulent local seafood imaginable—pan-seared snapper, perfectly grilled colossal shrimp, delicate conch fritters, and opulent lobster tails, each dish a symphony of Bahamian flavors. Every bite was a shared pleasure, every clink of glasses a toast to their newfound happiness and the sheer perfection of their escape.

But perhaps the most cherished ritual was their endless, romantic walks along the shoreline. The beaches of Nassau were not merely white; they were a breathtaking expanse of powdery, sugar-fine sand that glittered like scattered diamonds under the sun's benevolent gaze and the moon's soft luminescence. Hand-in-hand, they traversed miles of untouched coastline, the gentle, warm waves softly hissing and retreating at their bare feet, leaving ephemeral patterns in the pristine sand.

These strolls became their confessional, their quiet sanctuary, where each breath mingled with the ocean's murmur and dreams were spun into the salty air, each step further cementing their bond, and every kiss wasn't just a fleeting moments of passion, but significant declarations, each one a silent, fervent pledge that this love, born in stolen glances and nurtured by shared dreams, would truly last forever.

On their final day, the sun, though still bright, seemed to cast a melancholic glow over the lavish resort as Aileen and Michael began the bittersweet task of packing their luggage. Each shirt folded, each souvenir tucked away, felt like another second ticking off the clock of their blissful escape.

The honeymoon, a beautiful dream-come-true of turquoise waters and shared laughter, was over way too soon. Aileen sighed softly, a wistful sound, as she zipped shut her suitcase.

Michael, ever practical, double-checked under the bed and in the vanity drawers, ensuring no precious memory, no small trinket, was left behind. The silence in the now-sparsely furnished room was a stark contrast to the vibrant chatter and music that had filled their days.

With a final, lingering look at their private balcony, where so many mornings had begun with coffee and the endless expanse of the Atlantic, the couple descended to the hotel's breezy lobby. There, a waiting taxi, its engine idling softly, whisked them away.

The short ride back to the bustling Nassau International Airport was quieter than their arrival, punctuated only by the rumbling of the tires and the occasional glimpse of familiar landmarks flashing past – a vibrant market, a colorful row of houses – all now fading into the rearview mirror of memory.

The airport itself was a whirlwind of activity, a jarring reintroduction to the world outside their idyllic bubble. After navigating check-in and security, they boarded a small commuter plane. The propellers whirred to life with a familiar, slightly anxious hum, lifting them skyward. Below, the impossibly blue waters of the Bahamas gradually gave way to the deeper, grayer hues of the open ocean as they began their journey back to Miami, Florida. Aileen squeezed Michael's hand, a silent acknowledgment of the paradise they were leaving behind.

Upon landing in the sprawling Miami International Airport, the transition was immediate and jarring. The warm, laid-back atmosphere of Nassau was replaced by the cacophony of a major international hub – announcements blaring, people rushing, the stark glow of fluorescent lights.

They navigated the calm corridors with a sense of quiet determination in their steps until they reached their next gate. There, they transferred over to a much larger jet, its sleek, powerful engines promising a swifter, though less intimate, journey for the final leg to Portland, Maine.

As the plane taxied and then rocketed down the runway, Aileen leaned her head on Michael's shoulder, the hum of the engines a lullaby against the bittersweet pang of departure.

The long flight back home after their glorious honeymoon in Nassau brought with it a hard realization: they were now commencing their new lives together. The casual "we" of courtship had solidified into the weighty, wonderful "us" of marriage.

As they drove back to Applewood, a soft sigh escaped Aileen's lips, perhaps a complex mix of exhaustion from the long flight, a pang of wistful nostalgia, and a nascent understanding of what lay ahead. This wasn't just a return to their shared home; it was a return to *their* lives, now irrevocably intertwined.

The reality of shared bills, shared routines, shared decisions, and shared futures settled over them like the evening fog creeping in from the harbor. Their individual identities, once distinct and self-contained, had subtly shifted, becoming inextricably linked. They were no longer simply two individuals embarking on an adventure; they were a unit, a partnership, bound not just by vows exchanged at a church, but by an unspoken, weighty understanding that their futures, for better or worse, in sickness and in health, were singularly, permanently tied. It was a beautiful, terrifying, and utterly inescapable truth that now, as husband and wife, their stories would forever be written as one.

The weekend, stretching before them like a blank canvas, was their opportunity to settle into their new status, to unpack not just suitcases but the very essence of their shared future. They had just a few precious days to acclimate before returning to their routine jobs, their minds flushed with deep anticipation for the life ahead and a treasure trove of vivid memories they had forged over the past sun-drenched days.

Once they arrived back at their apartment, their newly wedded household, the familiar scent of home – a comforting blend of old books and their chosen candle selections – enveloped them as Michael turned the key in the lock.

Luggage thudded softly onto the living room rug, a stark contrast to the tiled floors of their resort suite. Together, they began the gentle ritual of unpacking, folding clothes still carrying the faint, sweet scent of sea air and sunscreen, carefully placing the few shells and woven trinkets they'd collected onto a shelf that now felt distinctly like 'theirs'.

With the last bag emptied and a comforting sense of order restored, Aileen reached for the telephone, her fingers trembling slightly with excitement. She dialed her family home, her voice bubbling with unconstrained joy as she announced their successful return to Applewood.

For the next thirty minutes, she painted a vibrant picture for her parents, recounting in vivid detail the many wonderful times in Nassau – the snorkeling, the delicious seafood, the breathtaking sunsets, the endless laughter. She specifically thanked her parents again, her voice thick with genuine gratitude, for their incredibly thoughtful and generous gift of paying for the wedding and reception, a gesture that had allowed them to begin their married life without a single worry.

Michael patiently waited for Aileen to finish her animated conversation, then took his turn. He phoned his dad, his voice warm with genuine happiness. He recapped the honeymoon to him, perhaps with fewer embellishments than Aileen but with no less affection, sharing the highlights, the adventures, and the overwhelming sense of peace and joy that had settled over them both.

As he hung up, a comfortable silence fell over their small apartment, broken only by the quiet hum of the refrigerator. They looked at each other, hand in hand, a silent promise passing between them – the adventure was truly just beginning.

The next day, the soft light of Saturday morning filtered gently through the bedroom curtains, painting the room in hues of soft gold. After a night steeped in the quiet joy of their newly sealed union – a night of whispered confidences, gentle affection, and peace of knowing they were finally home, together, as husband and wife – Aileen and Michael stirred simultaneously. There was no rush, no alarm clock, just the slow awakening into a shared space that now felt entirely their own. Michael pressed a soft kiss to Aileen's sleep-tousled hair, a silent acknowledgment of the new chapter that had truly begun.

Eventually, rising refreshed and invigorated, they moved through their new home with a leisurely grace. The aroma of freshly brewed coffee soon mingled with the scent of their shared morning. Over steaming mugs, they perched at the kitchen counter, a sense of purposeful anticipation bubbling beneath their peaceful exterior.

The refrigerator, a silent witness to their before-marriage chaos and the subsequent departure of most foodstuffs, stood starkly bare. It was a blank canvas, a symbol of their fresh start.

Michael pulled out a notepad and pen, and together, they began to make their first grocery list as a married couple. It quickly became a lively, collaborative effort, punctuated by laughter and the occasional playful debate about staples versus indulgence.

With their carefully crafted list in hand, they set off to the local supermarket, a mundane errand transformed into a goal in shared domesticity. The bustling aisles and cheerful cacophony of the store became the backdrop for their first real "negotiation" as a married pair.

Aileen, the disciplined firefighter, prioritized lean proteins, fresh seasonal produce, and whole grains – food to fuel demanding shifts and maintain peak physical condition. Michael, on the other hand, whose workday often demanded quick, comforting fixes and who harbored a fondness for artisan bread, sharper cheeses, and perhaps a clandestine bag of gourmet chips, advocated for items that spoke to his inner gourmand and his need for easy sustenance. There were good-natured jests about "rabbit food" versus "heart attack on a plate," but beneath the joking around, a genuine effort to understand and accommodate each other's needs prevailed.

They walked the line between healthy eating and comforting treats, between practical necessities and small luxuries, each finding a middle ground that ensured both their diets and their individual preferences would be satisfied. Their shopping cart, overflowing with a harmonious blend of their distinct tastes, was a testament to their successful collaboration.

This idyllic Saturday, however, was framed by the impending realities of their demanding professions. Aileen's duty shift at the fire station was scheduled to start early that

Sunday morning, pulling her away for a challenging, unpredictable twenty-four-hour shift.

Michael, on the other hand, was expected to be back behind his desk at the formidable bank building promptly on Monday morning, re-immersing himself in the world of high finance and complex transactions.

Their precious initial weekend as husband and wife, while filled with the promise of their new life, also served as a poignant reminder of the separate, vital roles they each played in the world, roles that would inevitably call them away from their safe romantic haven. They still had lots of things to do.

After an early, healthy yet satisfying, lunch of fresh salads and soups, Aileen and Michael chitchatted over their coffee, their conversation slowly shifting from daily pleasantries to a more practical matter. The apartment's layout, a persistent topic of discussion, was once again on the table, specifically the underutilized second bedroom. They pulled out a measuring tape, walked through the room, pacing out potential layouts, their heads close together in shared problem-solving.

After a thorough evaluation of the available square footage and a mental checklist of their evolving needs, a decision crystallized: they would convert the spare room, currently a repository for miscellaneous overflow, into a dynamic, multi-purpose space – a combination office and workout room. The idea sparked a shared sense of excitement and relief.

Fortunately, the rudimentary beginnings of a home gym already existed. A set of chrome dumbbells and a somewhat dusty yoga mat were tucked away in the back of the closet, remnants of Michael's New Year's Resolution from a few years prior. And Aileen's trusty, albeit currently garage-bound, treadmill, a sturdy model she hadn't wanted to part with, would fit perfectly along the longest wall, offering a window view during her morning runs. The vision was clear and invigorating.

There was, however, one glaring oversight in this otherwise perfect plan: the room was entirely devoid of any suitable furniture for the "office" component. No desk for a computer monitor and keyboard, no ergonomic chair for long work sessions, and certainly no bookcase or shelving to organize important manuals, paperwork, or reference materials. The room felt like a blank canvas, but one that desperately needed its essential strokes.

Recognizing the immediate need, Aileen and Michael wasted no time. A quick text to Michael's easygoing friend, Vince Drake, secured the loan of his well-maintained old pickup truck – a practical, no-frills vehicle perfect for hauling. With the keys in hand and a sense of purpose, they set off, the anticipation of their new project humming between them.

Their destination was Aileen's family home, a place filled with warmth and, hopefully, useful cast-offs. They needed to retrieve Aileen's treadmill and any other workout equipment her parents might have tucked away. Also, the old wooden bookcase in Aileen's bedroom would fit well in their new office space.

Upon their arrival, Aileen's parents greeted them with open arms and the comforting aroma of Faith's freshly baked cookies.

When Aileen explained their plan and inquired about the training equipment, her mother, ever the pragmatist, immediately said, "Sure! Anything to clear out the garage!" Her father, equally agreeable, added, "Happy to help you load it, too."

They worked as a cheerful team, carefully maneuvering the bulky treadmill, the weight bench, and a box of various resistance bands and smaller weights from the depths of her parents' meticulously organized garage into the bed of Vince's pickup. Groans and laughter mingled as they heaved the heavier items. They also managed to retrieve the bookcase from Aileen's bedroom.

As they paused, wiping their brows, a memory flickered in Aileen's mind, sparked by the conversation about furniture for their new office. "Dad," she began, "do you remember that old desk? The dark wood one I saw once in the attic, years ago?" The question hung in the air, a potential solution to their immediate furniture dilemma.

She vividly recalled the occasion. She had been a young teenager, perhaps thirteen or fourteen, when her dad had gone up to the rarely-visited attic to store an old, unused lamp that had seen better days. Curious and perpetually drawn to forgotten nooks, Aileen had followed him up the narrow, creaky wooden attic stairs.

Each step had groaned under her weight, echoing in the quiet, dusty space. As her eyes adjusted to the dim, filtered light that pierced through a small, grimy window, she remembered a world suspended in time.

Dust particles danced in the slivers of sunlight, illuminating a veritable treasure trove. She had noticed all sorts of vintage furniture – a stately, dark-wood dresser with ornate pulls, a velvet-clad armchair, a delicately carved side table, and, most prominently, a solid, old oak desk with deep, pull-out drawers.

Alongside these larger pieces, holiday decorations, still rested in their worn boxes, mingled with seasonal sporting equipment from bygone eras – battered ski boots, dusty tennis rackets, and a rusty croquet set. There was also a small, mismatched table with a single chair, stacks of weathered luggage, and countless cardboard boxes, tied with faded string or sealed with brittle tape, filled with who knew what forgotten treasures and mundane memories.

Climbing the rickety stairway, the attic door creaked open. The humid, musty air of the attic, thick with the scent of aged paper and forgotten things, hung heavy as Liam, Aileen, and Michael embarked on their mission. Their objective: to unearth that specific, long-dormant desk and chair, essential pieces for the nascent office and workout room taking shape in the newlywed's apartment. This wasn't a casual rummage; it was a targeted excavation, a hunt for furniture that held the promise of functionality and perhaps, a touch of nostalgia.

Deep within the shadowy recesses of the attic, nestled in a far corner that seemed to absorb the meager light, lay their prize. Underneath a quilt so aged and worn it might have been spun from dust itself, the desk waited. Its surface could tell years of neglect; it was shrouded in a thick blanket of dust particles.

As they gingerly approached, Michael, ever the observant one, noticed a partially opened drawer, revealing the delicate, almost architectural remnants of a mouse's abandoned nest – a tiny, poignant reminder of life's persistent presence even in forgotten spaces.

With a combined effort, Liam and Michael wrestled the wooden desk away from its hiding place and into the clearer, more open expanse of the attic. This allowed for a better appraisal of its condition. Aileen, her eyes alight with an immediate fondness, surveyed the piece. "This will be absolutely perfect," she declared, a smile gracing her lips. Her gaze then shifted, spotting the accompanying chair tucked away near a precarious stack of old cardboard boxes. "And look, the chair is over there," she pointed. "Both of these will do very nicely. Thanks, Dad!" she added with genuine gratitude, turning to Liam, her father, before reassuring him that a thorough cleaning and a good polish would transform the pair into ideal occupants of their new space.

While Liam and Michael, displaying amazing teamwork, began the laborious task of maneuvering the sturdy wooden desk and then the surprisingly manageable cushioned work chair down the narrow, creaking attic stairs, Aileen's curiosity took hold. Their destination was the waiting truck parked in the driveway, but in the interim, her objective was to indulge in a bit of exploration.

The attic was a realm defined by a single, meager beam. A solitary, bare incandescent light bulb, suspended precariously from a frayed wire, was the only defense against the encroaching gloom, casting long, grotesque shadows that writhed and danced with every subtle tremor of the loose floorboards. These shifting phantoms gave forgotten objects an ominous, fleeting life, while simultaneously accentuating the delicate, silvered lace of countless spiderwebs that clung like ancient flags to the rafters. The air hung heavy, thick with the scent of aged timber, forgotten paper, and a faint, sweet mustiness that spoke of decades of untouched items.

Her attention was inescapably drawn to a particularly prominent, almost imposing 'mountain' of small cardboard and wooden boxes set snugly under the sloping eaves. What distinguished this towering heap was not merely its size, but its remarkable order; it seemed, upon closer inspection, to have been meticulously arranged, a proof of someone's careful preservation.

The majority of these containers held a myriad of personal belongings: old faded sepia photographs, some with curling edges and unknown faces; dainty knitted gloves and scarves, still retaining the faintest hint of lavender or cedar; ornate brooches with missing stones; and a sundry of other family keepsakes – pressed flowers, a child's first tooth, a small, worn leather-bound diary. Each item felt like a quiet secret from a bygone generation.

Among this collection, her discerning eye caught sight of a small, vintage, intricately engraved wooden box. Its dark wood, polished smooth by time and countless touches, gleamed with an heirloom quality, secured by a tiny, tarnished brass clasp. Aileen's heart gave a little jolt when she saw the delicate, looping script of its label, clearly addressed to her mother: "To Faith, From Mom."

Intrigued, a sense of curiosity bubbling within her, Aileen carefully, almost reverently, lifted the hinged lid. Inside, instead of jewels, lay a true treasure trove of forgotten papery memories: a dense stack of letters, a scatter of colorful, if faded, postcards, and numerous short, hastily scribbled notes. Their dates spanned a remarkable breadth, beginning long before Aileen's own birth and extending well into her childhood – a silent, tangible chronicle of a life lived, loved, and now, waiting to be rediscovered.

Upon closer scrutiny, the meticulous arrangement continued within the box itself. The letters, postcards, and notes had been systematically bundled by year, each stack tied with a small, colorful piece of yarn – now faded to pastel rainbows – a testament to the tender care with which they had been cataloged. Aileen, her fingers trembling slightly with a mixture of excitement and reverence, began to study each stack one by one. She soon discovered that every single item in this precious box was a loving remembrance saved by her grandmother, Nora Kelly, and given to her mother, Faith, long ago.

The early years chronicled in the first bundles revealed the innocent hopes and declared affections of a blossoming romance between her mother and father before they were married – letters hinting at blushing courtships and whispered promises.

Some bundles held yellowed, elegantly scripted wedding invitations, along with correspondence from her aunts and uncles, keepsakes of family life: congratulatory notes, annual Christmas cards adorned with festive, if dated, scenes, and heartfelt holiday wishes that painted vivid snapshots of bygone celebrations.

15

Affirmation

The final, and most poignant, collection was composed exclusively of letters from her grandmother, Nora Kelly, to her daughter, Faith, all were dated subsequent to the year Aileen was born. As she carefully unfurled these, Aileen felt an unusual sense of connection, a chilling realization that she was reading words specifically written with *her* in mind, even if indirectly.

Each letter, penned in her grandmother's steady, loving hand, revealed Nora's deepest, most tender hopes for her granddaughter's future, her quiet fears for life's inevitable dangers and heartbreaks, and her longing to guide Aileen, through her daughter, Faith, with unseen advice and to protect her in every way a grandmother's love could reach across time and distance, forming an eternal, sacred trust.

The crisp, aged paper, yellowed with the passage of time and bearing the faint scent of dried lavender and memory, crackled softly beneath Aileen's trembling fingers. Each rustle was a whisper from the past as she absorbed the words Nana, her beloved grandmother had penned to her daughter, Faith – words meant for Aileen's eyes now, a legacy entrusted to her care. It wasn't mere nostalgia that made her breath hitch; it was the intricate tapestry of love woven into each heartfelt sentence, revealing subtle yet significant details that resonated deep within her.

Beyond the familiar, comforting slant of Nana's Script, a distinctive handwriting that Aileen had traced countless times in her youth, lay something else entirely, a secret language that spoke directly to her soul.

Nestled beside every mention of her own name, "Aileen," a tiny, hand-drawn smiley face peeked out from the ink. These weren't just any doodles; they were the exact, endearingly quirky caricatures Nana had etched onto the margins of Aileen's childhood drawings, a sort of secret code of joy, a shred of shared laughter and whispered confidences. It was as if Nana's playful spirit, her irrepressible zest for life, had found a way to punctuate her loving words with these familiar, whimsical marks, a signature of her enduring presence.

Aileen's thoughts, as if guided by an unseen force, also returned to the precious smiley face drawing Nana had secretly passed to her during her days in the nursing home, her health failing but her spirit undimmed. That day, Aileen had carefully stored it in her most treasured keepsake box that day, a ritual of love and remembrance. That very box, now holding this correspondence, was placed in a prominent spot on the bedroom closet shelf, a beacon of Nana's enduring love within her wedded home.

Then came the passage that truly made Aileen's breath stumble, a sentence that seemed to shimmer with an inner light, rewriting her understanding of her own existence. Nana had noted in this particular letter, her words imbued with a tender warmth, "I'm so happy, and proud that you, Faith, and Liam brought such a beautiful, joyful, and spirited girl into the world." The words hit her deeply, a wave of unconditional pride and love washing over Aileen, a feeling so potent it brought tears to her eyes. This was not just a declaration of affection; it was an affirmation of her very being, a validation of the spirit Nana had always seen within her.

At that very moment, the full weight of Nana's enduring love and her subtle, almost imperceptible, guidance descended upon Aileen like a gentle, warm embrace. It wasn't a sudden, jarring revelation, but a slow, dawning of understanding, like the gradual unfolding of a delicate blossom. Nana's passing, Aileen now grasped with a certainty that settled deep in her bones, hadn't been an ending, but a beautiful, graceful transformation.

Nana's spirit, no, her very soul, had been liberated from the confines of her earthly body, free to continue watching over her beloved granddaughter, to embrace and protect her from realms unseen, her love a boundless, invisible guiding shield.

The cryptic warnings of the past, the gentle nudges in a particular direction that had often felt like inexplicable intuition, the almost imperceptible influences that had shaped her choices and guided her path – they all coalesced, the scattered pieces of a grand design now undeniably clear.

They were not mere coincidences, not the random twists of fate. They were Nana's invisible hand, a loving, guiding presence, her spectral touch ever-present, a murmur leading her steps along her way, ensuring she navigated life's currents with grace and resilience.

As Aileen, her voice thick with emotion, finally read the last of Nana's letters aloud, the words seemed to shimmer with an ethereal light, as if infused with Nana's very essence.

And then, as if conjuring her presence from the very air, a faint, familiar whisper, soft as a summer breeze yet undeniably Nana's, brushed against her ear, sending a shiver down her spine. *"I will always be with you. Aileen."* The message, delivered not just through ink on paper but through a spectral caress, a tangible manifestation of love beyond the veil, cemented the connection that transcended even death, a bond unbreakable by time or space.

Clutching the letters, the whispers of Nana's love still echoing in her heart, a rush of tears welled up in her eyes as the implications of this revelation hit her deep within her very soul. It was a cleansing, a release of years of grief mingled with the overwhelming joy of renewed connection.

Aileen, now finally at peace with the loss of her grandmother, her heart lighter than it had been in years, wiped her tears. She acknowledged Nana's presence not just in the letters, but in the very air around her, a silent promise fulfilled. She gathered all the letters back into the wooden box, and with a newfound serenity, slowly descended the attic stairs, each step carrying her closer to the tangible world, but with Nana forever a part of her internal landscape.

Once on the brightly lit main floor of the house, her father greeted her, his brow furrowed with concern at the sight of her swollen eyes. "Aileen, honey, is everything alright?" he asked, his voice filled with gentle worry.

She offered him a fleeting, radiant grin, a reflection of the peace that had settled within her. "Yes, Dad," she replied, her voice steady and clear, imbued with a quiet strength. "Everything's going to be just fine." And for the first time in a long time, she truly believed it.

After a heartfelt exchange of gratitude with her father for his invaluable help, Michael and Aileen redirected their attention to the return ride back to their tenement building. The day's arduous task was far from over, and the borrowed pickup truck, generously lent to them by Vince, was laden with their newly acquired treasures.

With a shared sigh, a blend of exertion and anticipation, they commenced the slow, deliberate process of unloading the truck's numerous contents. Each item, from the treadmill to the sturdy desk, the bookcase, and the comforting chair, was carefully wrestled from the truck bed and then carried on the laborious journey inside.

The tenement's narrow, echoing stairwell became their temporary battleground. Trip after trip, they ascended the steps to their second-floor apartment, the weight of the furniture and boxes pressing down on their arms and legs. The shared grunts of effort punctuated the rhythm of their ascent and descent.

These were not swift, energetic actions, but rather slow and steady, proving their determination, interspersed with much-needed pauses. They'd stop on the landings, leaning against the cool brick walls, their chests pounding, before pushing onward. Small sips from a water bottle, their re-hydration routine, became welcome respites, fueling them for the next leg of their conveyance. Finally, after what felt like an eternity of stair-climbing and muscle-aching, the last item was deposited inside their roomy apartment.

The focal point of their immediate attention was the desk. Michael set to work with a small rag and a can of polish, coaxing a renewed luster from its surface. Aileen, meanwhile, knelt to examine a leg that had proclaimed its slight instability. With a few practiced turns of a screwdriver, its wobble was silenced, its sturdiness restored. Once satisfied, they maneuvered the desk into its designated spot, a previously empty corner that now seemed poised for the purpose.

The cushioned chair, a welcome addition for countless hours of work and contemplation, was then positioned alongside it. And the bookcase was placed along one wall. A collective exhale, and a shared look of contentment passed between them. "Perfect," they echoed in unison, the simple word carrying the weight of their accomplishment.

Aileen then turned her attention to a more personal acquisition. She carefully retrieved the intricately carved wooden box she found in the attic, the repository of Nana's cherished letters. With a gentle touch, she placed it on the closet shelf, nestling it beside another precious item – her own childhood keepsake box, a vessel holding fragments of her past. The connection was poignant; Nana's wisdom and

Aileen's nascent memories, now side by side, were a tangible representation of legacy and personal history intertwined.

With all the essential pieces of their new workspace now firmly in place in what would also serve as a workout room, a palpable exhaustion settled over Michael and Aileen. The physical demands of the day, compounded by the emotional weight of unpacking memories, had taken their toll.

Understanding each other's fatigue without a word, they decided to prepare a light, yet nourishing, late dinner together. The simple act of chopping vegetables and stirring a pot offered a gentle, comforting end to their laborious day.

Afterward, they sought solace on their stuffed sofa in the living room, fully intending to unwind by watching a couple of shows on television. However, the overwhelming weariness, a deep, bone-tired sensation, had already claimed them. The flickering images on the screen faded into a hazy blur as their eyelids grew heavy, signaling an undeniable readiness for the deep, restorative sleep they so desperately needed.

The next day loomed large on their combined schedules, not just as the end of the weekend, but as the day Aileen dons her gear once again. It will be her inaugural duty shift back at the fire station, a significant milestone following the unforgettable celebration of her wedding and the subsequent idyllic honeymoon spent basking in the tropical splendor of Nassau. The familiar routines of the station, the shared anticipation of calls, and the quick-paced camaraderie will be a world away from the tranquil shores she recently shared with Michael.

Michael, on the other hand, will enjoy a brief reprieve, one sole day of freedom from professional demands, allowing him an earned chance to unwind and truly recuperate before plunging back into his tough work routine. His suit and tie will have to wait one more day.

The muffled silence of the early hour clung to the bedroom, broken only by the rhythmic, deep breathing of the man beside her. Aileen drifted slowly out of a deep sleep, her mind surfacing through layers of comfortable warmth. It was still pre-dawn, the room cast in a cool, pearl-gray light that promised the imminent arrival of Sunday.

Aileen sluggishly turned onto her side, finding herself facing Michael. He was sprawled on his back, utterly motionless, a testament to yesterday's grueling workout session. His broad shoulders were visible above the covers, and a sheaf of rich brown hair had fallen across his forehead. She reached out a hand, hesitating just a moment before gently sweeping the errant strands away from his temple. A soft smile touched her lips—a silent acknowledgment of their secure world—and then, with the practiced stealth of a light sleeper, she rolled away, pivoting her legs off the mattress.

Her phone lay face down on the nightstand. The alarm, set for 5:30 AM, hadn't yet begun its insistent chime, but Aileen knew she was only minutes away from it. She grabbed the phone and silenced the setting before the digital noise could shatter Michael's peace.

Standing up, she felt the cool air momentarily shock her calves before she slid her feet into the plush, worn safety of her favorite fleece slippers. She shuffled silently across the carpet, snatching her heavy, flannel bathrobe from the hook behind the door.

With utmost care, she turned the door handle and eased it shut, ensuring the soft *click* of the latch was the only sound. Michael was afforded his rest; she needed this quiet, focused time to prepare for her first day back on shift duty after her marriage and honeymoon.

The kitchen was the warmest room in the apartment, and the first scent that greeted her was residual nutmeg and cinnamon from last night. Aileen set up the drip coffee maker, savoring the low burble and hiss as the machine began its sacred morning ritual.

While the rich, dark liquid brewed, she stood at the window, staring out at the slowly awakening town. The sky was transforming from inky velvet to a vibrant spectrum of golds and soft oranges, pushing back the shadows clinging to the high-rises around her. It was a beautiful, powerful transition, mirroring the transition she was about to make herself.

When the pot was full, Aileen poured herself a deep mug of steaming coffee, its aroma a bracing tonic. She hastily assembled a breakfast sandwich—two slices of whole wheat bread, a smear of butter, a fried egg, and a slice of sharp cheddar—and consumed it along with a handful of her morning vitamins, washing everything down with the hot, slightly bitter caffeine. Every move was efficient, driven by the professional clock in her mind.

A glance at the rectangular wall clock above the stove confirmed her timing: 6:05 AM. Just enough time for a fast, cleansing rinse before the necessity of the commute to the fire substation.

The bathroom door clicked shut, and she stepped beneath the cascade of scalding water, letting the steam envelop her. The warmth chased away the last vestiges of sleep and reset her nervous system from relaxed spouse to vigilant firefighter. After vigorously toweling her skin until it was pink and tingling, she wrapped the large cotton towel securely around herself.

With a sigh of contentment, she reached for her familiar toothbrush, its bristles worn just so. A dollop of minty paste, the taste a vibrant promise of freshness, filled her mouth as she began the rhythm of cleaning. The cool, invigorating sensation spread across her tongue and gums with each stroke, a ritualistic cleansing that washed away the lingering remnants of the day before. Finally, she tipped her head back, the sharp, clean scent of the mouthwash filling her nostrils as she swished, the minty tide leaving her breath as pure and bright as a winter morning.

She stood before the fogging mirror, brushing her thick, red hair with swift, practiced strokes, then gathered the bulk of it and twisted it into a tight, practical bun at the nape of her neck.

Just as she was reaching for the can of hairspray, a gentle rap came at the door.

"I'm up now, Aileen, good morning!" Michael's voice, husky and deep with sleep, announced from the hallway.

Aileen smiled; the sound of his voice was a comfort. "Good morning, Michael. You were out cold when I got up this morning."

"Yeah, I was beat," he admitted, the sound of his slippers shuffling barely audible outside the door. "But I slept really well, you?"

"Yup, but the clock is ticking for me," she replied, her tone shifting toward professional readiness. "I gotta be on duty soon."

She slipped back into the bedroom, closing the door behind her to afford the necessary privacy for the transformation. With deliberate care, she began donning the components of her fire department uniform.

First, the dark blue utility pants, crisp and starched. Then, the light blue short-sleeved shirt—the fabric felt sturdy and familiar against her skin. Finally, her highly polished, but slightly scuffed, black leather work shoes, tied tightly for the long hours ahead.

Making her way over to her dresser, she stood before the mirror, giving herself the once-over. This was the moment of complete transition. She precisely attached her silver name pin on the left side and the distinctive, gleaming silver fire department badge onto the right side of her shirt, positioning them exactly one inch above each pocket flap. The badge felt cool and heavy, a symbol of service and trust.

Her eyes drifted to her left hand, where her wedding band caught the reflected light. A wide, heartfelt smile blossomed on her face as she gazed at the simple golden ring etched with forget-me-not flowers. The memories flooded back: the perfect, sunny day of their marriage ceremony and the awesome, carefree days of their honeymoon spent on the warm, turquoise beaches of Nassau. The badge might represent her career, but the ring represented her real foundation.

Aileen gathered her car keys and turned to leave. In the main room, Michael was settled at the kitchen table, looking relaxed in shorts and a T-shirt, enjoying a large bowl of cereal, buttered toast, and his own cup of coffee. He was humming a low, tuneless melody to himself, the picture of domestic tranquility and peace.

As Aileen stepped toward the exit, Michael rose instantly. He met her near the doorway, his eyes warm and approving as he took in her sharp, ready appearance. He pulled her into a loving, lingering hug, grounding her for a moment in the physical reality of their life together, before offering a gentle, tender kiss.

He opened the apartment door for her. "Go get 'em, girl!" he said, his voice full of pride.

Aileen stepped out into the hallway, the professional focus settling firmly over her anticipation. The weight of her duties, and the memory of her late Nana's constant, guiding presence—her letters, her unwavering belief in Aileen's strength, her simple mantra of perseverance—rose up inside of her. Aileen raised her head slightly, her gaze fixed on the ceiling, a silent promise uttered to the spirit that had shaped her resolve.

"We sure will, Michael!" she called back, her voice firm and full of purpose.

Michael stood in the doorway, watching his wife's purposeful stride carry her down the corridor. He waited until she made the final corner and disappeared down the stairs, ready to begin the challenging, exhilarating rest of her life, confident, guided, and unafraid.

16

Epilogue

The culmination of years of relentless dedication was realized when Aileen, heralded for her uncompromised discipline, strategic thinking, and commitment to leadership, formally advanced to the rank of Lieutenant within the highly respected Applewood Fire Department. Her promotion was not merely a ceremonial step but a practical acknowledgment of her ability to manage high-stakes situations. She immediately took command of Engine Three's crew, shaping them into a cohesive, rapidly responsive unit known for their precision and calm under pressure.

Beyond the daily demands of responding to calls, Aileen dedicated substantial time to operational improvement. Drawing on her extensive experience, she spearheaded the development of several new and highly innovative first-aid and advanced trauma stabilization procedures—protocols that emphasized rapid assessment and efficient field triage. These procedures, championed by Aileen and rigorously tested, were eventually ratified by the regional health council and integrated as mandatory components of the department's continuing education curriculum, fundamentally improving patient outcomes across the jurisdiction.

The spiritual guidance that had once been a constant force in Aileen's life—the perpetual guiding voice and wisdom of her beloved Nana—softened into a deeply internalized intuition. It was no longer an external directive but a gentle echo, a sense of self-trust rooted deep in her heart. Yet, when exhaustion threatened to overwhelm her or when a life-or-death decision hung in the balance, Aileen could still perceive, or feel, the faint, comforting warmth of Nana's whisper, a final, ethereal reassurance that had guided her through her foundation years.

Amidst her demanding career, Aileen and Michael, established a solid, prosperous domestic foundation. Michael had settled comfortably into his role as Vice President of Operations at the regional bank, earning a sterling reputation for his meticulous accuracy, financial aptitude, and calm diplomacy.

One crisp autumn morning, the Brown family household expanded dramatically with the joyous, though chaotic, arrival of identical twin baby girls, fiery redheads who inherited their mother's determination and their father's observant nature. Named Rose and Willow, the twins quickly became the singular focus of their parents, who proved to be exceptionally devoted and loving. Aileen and Michael meticulously instilled in their daughters the same values of intellectual curiosity, respect, and community service that had defined their own lives.

Meanwhile, Aileen's father, Liam, having dedicated over thirty years to battling blazes and rescuing citizens, retired from the fire service with dignity. His dedication afforded him a substantial and comfortable pension, allowing him to trade the adrenaline-fueled pace of the station for the pleasant quiet of home life. He and his wife, Faith, initially indulged in the well-deserved respite, celebrating their freedom with a luxurious second honeymoon to the tropical splendor of Maui, Hawaii, where they rediscovered the simple joy of uninterrupted togetherness.

Soon, however, the quiet became too deep. Liam, whose life had been defined by service, began to crave a familiar sense of purpose and structure. Seeking a meaningful, low-stress connection to the community, he successfully trained for and earned his school bus driver's license endorsement. He was promptly hired by the regional school system and assigned the challenging route of transporting elementary through high school students. He discovered that the daily morning and afternoon interactions—the cheerful chaos, the budding personalities, and the trust placed in him—were significantly refreshing and uplifting, cementing his role as a beloved, steady presence in the students' lives.

Faith found a joyful and satisfying outlet in her kitchen, rediscovering her prodigious talent for baking. Her pies, scones, cookies, and handcrafted breads were renowned among family and neighbors.

Encouraged by Liam, she soon branched out, supplying her prized baked goods to the specialty section of the local supermarket. Demand quickly outstripped her home kitchen's capacity, leading her and Liam to eventually invest in opening a charming, dedicated space called "Faith's Flourishes."

Situated in the revitalized waterfront business district, the shop initially opened only for the bustling summer season. However, the unique aroma of cinnamon and yeast, coupled with Faith's delicious confections, drew such a loyal following that it soon became obvious they needed to expand their hours, transforming "Faith's Flourishes" into a thriving, year-round bakery establishment.

The Byrne family's younger generation also flourished. Sean, after committing himself to higher education, earned his Bachelor's degree in Secondary Education with a specialization in History. He subsequently moved north out of the family residence and secured a coveted teaching position at the middle school in the historic town of Bath, Maine. Known for his engaging classroom style and patience, he quickly became a valuable asset to the faculty and a popular, respected mentor among the students, effortlessly navigating the complexities of adolescent education.

Maya Fielding, Aileen's steadfast friend, successfully graduated from nursing school with high honors. She accepted a highly demanding role as a floor nurse on the critical care unit at the large regional hospital in Garrison. Despite their professional responsibilities and the miles separating them, the deep connection forged during their formative years remained unbroken; Maya and Aileen maintained a dedicated friendship, relying on weekly video calls and shared dinners to stay connected to this very day.

Finally, Georgia, Aileen's spirited friend from the fire academy, chose to seek her career further up the coast shortly after their graduation. She was successfully hired by the Boothbay Harbor Fire Department, finding the coastal environment and the demands of serving a major tourist destination both exhilarating and rewarding. She easily integrated into the tight-knit community, enjoying the lively social life and the constant influx of activity characteristic of that bustling maritime region.

The End

Acknowledgment

Writing a first book can be a daunting challenge for a greenhorn author like me.

This story has been in the back of my head for several years, and the summer of 2025 provided me with the time off to actually sit down and let it flow.

I want to extend my heartfelt thanks to my wonderful wife, Cheryl, who put up with my long days and evenings behind the keyboard.

Her patience and support have been, and will always be, appreciated.

I'd like to recognize Parker Publishers for their dedicated assistance and guidance throughout this process. They helped make this formidable adventure a reality.

Finally, a sincere thanks to you, the reader, for letting me tell my story.

About the Author

Don D. Boucher grew up in Auburn, Maine, with his parents, Alice and Cecil Boucher, along with his older sister, Jackie. He attended Sacred Heart Elementary School and subsequently graduated from Edward Little High School in 1969.

From a very young age, he has enjoyed a variety of sports, including baseball, hockey, skiing, ice skating, and hiking. He delighted in reading classic books and dreamed of becoming an author one day. In high school, Don joined a rock-and-roll band, playing rhythm guitar and, on occasion, bass. To this day, he enjoys listening to classic rock.

Over the years, Don has held many diverse occupations, including housekeeping at a local medical center and as a delivery driver for the local Budweiser distributor.

In 1977, after completing the written and physical tests, Don was hired as a firefighter for the Lewiston Fire Department, where he honorably served the community. After working there for 25 years, he subsequently retired, having reached the rank of lieutenant.

While serving as a firefighter and afterwards, he designed and maintained Websites for various organizations in Maine, honing his digital skills in communication and graphics.

After retirement, he drove for a wheelchair van company based in Lewiston, delivering patients to and from appointments throughout south-central Maine.

Through the years, Don and his wife, Cheryl, have owned numerous sail and motor boats that they used to cruise the majestic Maine seacoast, spending nights securely anchored at protected anchorages and harbors along the way. They have also owned many Harley-Davidson motorcycles, with which they enjoyed touring northern New England.

In 2007, he and his wife moved from Lewiston to the quiet village of Greene, Maine, with their daughter, Susan.

In 2011, Don received training, earned his passenger and school bus license endorsements, and got a job driving a school bus for Hudson Bus Lines in Lewiston. He has been driving Lewiston students of all ages to and from school for over 15 years now.

His daily 2-way interactions with his students and his listening to their thoughts and dreams were what sparked the idea to tell Aileen's story. It comes straight from his heart.